Contents

'No mother is ever, completely, a child's idea of what a mother should be, and I suppose it works the other way around as well. But despite everything, we didn't do badly by one another, we did as well as most.'

Margaret Atwood,
The Handmaid's Tale

Foreword

FOREWORD

You cannot ignore the relationship you have with your mother. Unlike most relationships with fathers, words and feelings flow abundantly. Is the fictional mother at all like the real thing? Can the real mother be as perfect as Mrs March in *Little Women* and Mother in *The Railway Children*? Are daughters in fiction more unrealistically perfect too? Bobby in *The Railway Children* has her 'power of silent sympathy — able to know that you are unhappy, to love you extra on that account, without bothering you by telling you all the time how sorry she is for you'. Are writers today likely to create such wonderfully loving and sensitive mothers and daughters?

Eighty-six years after *The Railway Children* first appeared, it may come as a surprise to find that the stories in *Mother's Day* do display an enormous amount of tenderness between mother and daughter. It is surprising because of what has happened to women in between and the revolution that has happened in the family. Children are no longer to obey, respect and love in a one-way traffic with no right to expect anything much more than protection from their parents. Girls have been educated to answer back and to determine the course of their lives. But these ten stories, while they reflect so many of the moods of the special relationship, are all about the fundamental love that exists between mother and daughter, daughter and mother, the good intentions of mothers that can seem unwelcome at times to the daughters, who see them as thwarting, frustrating but not loving.

There are laughter and truths in Anne Fine's story, there are misunderstandings and tears and then understanding in Berlie Doherty's, there is a mother's ability to change in Vivien Alcock's, there are rebellion and reconciliation in Jamila Gavin's and Gwen Grant's. Marjorie Darke shows the friendship and the complex tugs of love. There is welcome discovery in Annie Dalton's, while Monica Hughes shows how a high-tech mother/daughter relationship has its traditional core. There are embarrassment and loyalty in Jean Ure's, and Jacqueline Wilson shows how mums need their girls and girls need their mums.

Is the relationship so special, perhaps, because the instinct to mother one's daughter and mother one's mother seems to survive every onslaught? Is it perhaps because your mother is your future in a way your father cannot be? You can and very likely will share the same experiences. Whatever the reason, it is a relationship of many moods as these writers richly convey, and one that shapes your future.

Very Different

ANNE FINE

'Mum,' I said. 'Tell me the story of how you were born.'

'I've told you before.'

'So tell me again.'

She wasn't busy. She was just sitting on the sofa behind me, disapproving while I did my eyes with my new aubergine stuff. I could see her in the mirror.

'Get on with it, then,' I ordered. 'I'm off out soon.'

'Then you haven't time to hear it all over again.'

'Yes, I have.'

To prove it, I dropped down on the rug in a perfect lotus, my back completely straight. She didn't send me to all those ballet lessons for nothing. Mum made a face. She hates it when I do that. She says it makes her feel a hundred years old.

'Go on, then,' I told her, and reached for the nail polish bottles. I'd bought them that morning. They were lovely. Smoked glass, and shaped like roly-poly little moonmen. I stood them by my bare feet, tiny fat sentries, while I did my toes. They didn't have any labels. To tell what colour the polish was, you had to look into their big round eyes. The one by my left foot had apple green eyes, and the one by my right foot had silver.

'You take care not to drip that stuff over the carpet,' Mum nagged me.

'Get on with the *story*,' I told her. 'How you were born.'

'You told me you were leaving at seven to see a film about weevils taking over the Falklands.'

'Not weevils,' I said. 'Giant cockroaches. And not the Falklands, either. The Channel Islands. Out of season.'

'*You're* out of season,' Mum scolded. She meant my dress. And there's not that much to it, I have to admit. Dad won't even let me wear it when I'm at his house. He says I might just as well go about stark naked. Mum's not that keen on it, either. She sighs and says there's no point *saying* anything. Then she goes on to say it all the same. But I still wear the dress.

'If you don't get on with the story right now,' I warned, 'I'll wear it without the shoulder straps.'

Mum hates it when I wear it without the shoulder straps. She thinks it will fall off if I sneeze. She got on with the story pretty sharpish.

'Your granny and grandpa had known one another for a number of years. They started courting seriously on bonfire night one year. And it was only a matter of time, a year at most, before they became very close.'

I kept my head down over my shining toes and shook my hair around my face, but she still caught me grinning.

'Listen,' she said. 'This is your grandparents we're talking about. My father and mother. Things were different then. Very different.'

'You're telling me,' I chortled. I *love* this story.

Mum simply decided to ignore me.

'Both of them thought, right from the very start, that they would get married some day. And they were very much in love, so, as I said, they became close.'

'*Very* close, you said.'

'Very close, then.'

I stopped painting my toes. We were getting to one of the best bits.

'Nevertheless,' said Mum, 'they were always most careful to take full precautions.'

I can't help it if I start laughing, can I? It's so *funny*. 'I *love* the way you say that,' I told her. '"Take full precautions".' I rolled the words around my mouth. 'Like rubber pads and plastic gloves and woolly vests and quarantine.' Suddenly I noticed the clock hands, and broke off.

'Go *on*,' I ordered her sternly. 'We haven't got much longer.'

Mum took up the tale with as much dignity as she could muster, pretending she'd never been interrupted.

'So when it became clear that something had gone wrong, they were really shaken and upset. Your grandpa, George, especially. You see, he hadn't really planned on marrying for years, let alone having a baby. George had great dreams, then, for getting just a little bit more experience at Waverley's, then going out to the Persian Gulf, or somewhere, and making his name in a small but expanding engineering firm he'd been told about. And Granny had plans, too, to use a little money her Great Aunt Doe had left her, and open a tiny quilt shop on Ware Street. It was going to be called

11

The Peaceable Kingdom. She'd even designed her own shop sign. It was lovely.'

Her voice trailed off. I know she was remembering the day her mother found the old design inside the pages of a book.

'Poor Granny,' I said. 'Poor Grandpa.'

I meant it. I honestly wasn't just having her on. I don't know why she had to give me that suspicious look before she carried on.

'So they asked a friend for advice, and he gave them the name of this man – a doctor – '

'The friend! Don't miss out the friend! I *love* the seedy friend bit!' But I had to check the clock, and it was too late, I could tell. 'No,' I said. 'It's too near seven. You'll have to skip the seedy friend. We don't have time for him today.'

Mum shook her head in wonder. I think she sometimes thinks she's raised a monster.

'So the next day George and Ellie went off to see this doctor. George was apparently in a dreadful mood. He wouldn't even hold Ellie's hand. He barely spoke. The doctor's name was Fowler, Dr Charles Fowler. He lived in a lovely old house, one of the ones they uprooted to make way for that nasty new Tesco's. His waiting room was up a lot of steps. It was a white waiting room, and unheated. Your granny said she felt quite cold.'

'Shiver, shiver!' (I, of course, know what's coming next.)

'And although they were the only people in there, it was at least half an hour before the receptionist showed them into the surgery. Dr Fowler apologised for keeping them waiting, and asked them both to sit down. He even drew out a chair for Ellie. Then he walked round and sat at the other side of his desk, about as close as you are to me right now.'

I sat quite, quite still. This is the best bit.

'They both liked him enormously, right from the start. He was very sympathetic, very professional. Fatherly, I suppose. He asked after Ellie's dates, and then he wanted to know if there were any other symptoms. He checked on everything, every small detail. He was so careful. He said they might not believe it, but some doctors made a tidy living on the side "helping out" young women who thought, quite mistakenly, that they were pregnant.

'And he was perfectly frank and open about money. He said that since the two of them had been sensible enough to seek help without delay, he would only have to charge them seventy pounds, which was the very minimum, payable in advance, with absolutely no extras at all. He said that he could almost guarantee that there would be no complications. Ellie was obviously a healthy young woman. And although she would have to go overnight into a special nursing home, that was really just to be extra careful, since it was actually a very simple operation.

'Ellie could see that George was most impressed with him. I think they'd both thought that, since the whole business was so forbidden and illegal, they'd have to deal with a very different type. Very different. So George nodded, and Ellie nodded, and Dr Fowler nodded. And then, when everyone had nodded round at everyone else, Dr Fowler said he'd see what he could do to fix the whole business up quickly, so a nice couple like them didn't have to sit around worrying themselves sick about when it would be.'

You watch Mum's face when she tells this bit.

'So then Dr Fowler picked up the telephone on his desk and started to dial the number of the nursing home, while George and Ellie smiled bravely at one another and felt better about things than they had in a fortnight. But the nursing home took its time answering. The room was quiet, not even a clock ticking, and they could hear the ringing tone quite clearly, even though Dr Fowler was holding the receiver to his ear.'

She stopped. She always stops at this bit. It's so weird.

'Go on,' I said. 'And then – '

'And then someone answered – at least, that's what they thought, of course, because Dr Fowler began to speak. "Hello, Matron. How are you? . . . Well, that's good . . . Fine. Now listen, Matron. I have a young couple with me here now who have just got themselves into a bit of a fix," – and here he winked across your grandmother's head at George.'

'Pig!' I whispered. I *hate* old Dr Fowler at this bit. I just *hate* him. 'Sexist pig!'

'And just at that moment, as he was winking at your grandfather, the two of them heard the ringing tone again, faint but perfectly clear, coming out of the earpiece of the receiver.'

'Brrrrrrrr-brrrrrrrrrrrr.' (I always do this bit for her.)

'Brrrrrrrr-brrrrrrrrrrrr.' Creepy!

'And your granny looked across at George, and George looked back at her. He had heard it too, you see. And she says she remembers putting her hands across her stomach – '

'Across *you*.'

'Well, yes. As it later turned out. Across me. And she remembers that she thought: "Oh, well".'

'Just that? "Oh, well"?' (I find this bit so hard to believe. But that's what Mum always says Granny always told her.)

'Yes. Just, "Oh, well". She says she couldn't think any further, not just then, for all the time that frightful man was chatting away into the telephone: "You mean you actually have a spare bed there right now, Matron? . . . A sudden cancellation? . . . Well, that would be perfect. Shall we settle for four o'clock, then? . . . Fine . . . Fine." And all through, in the pauses, they could still hear that tiny ringing going on and on and on.'

'Oooooh!' I can hardly bear to think about it. It sends the shivers all over me. 'Ooooooh!'

'Then George stood up and held out his hand to Ellie, and both of them walked straight out of the surgery, just like that, without a word. They left Dr Fowler sitting behind his desk with the receiver in his hand still giving off those telltale little sounds. And they went through the empty waiting room, and down the stairs to the street, where George turned to Ellie and said: "I suppose that's curtains for the Persian Gulf, then," and Ellie nodded, feeling a bit sorry about the quilt shop, too. So they walked straight into the first restaurant they saw and bought a simply wonderful supper with some of the money George had borrowed that morning to pay the doctor.'

'And they never thought of asking around again?'

'It was difficult in those days. It was completely and totally against the law. If you got caught, you went to prison.'

'And so they just got married.'

'Yes.'

'And you were born seven months later.'

'That's right.'

'Amazing. It's absolutely *amazing*,' I said. (I always do.)

'I don't see why, particularly,' says Mum. (She always does.) 'That's how things *were*, back then.'

And I try to explain.

'All those *dreams*,' I say. 'All those *plans*. Grandpa's Persian Gulf, and Granny's Peaceable Kingdom. All up in smoke, just like that. Ending up married with a baby, just because of a ringing tone.' I give myself a little shake. 'It could *never* happen nowadays.'

'I told you,' Mum says. 'Things were different then. Very different.'

The clock struck seven. I had to go. I hate missing the start of a film. I rose and put the two roly-poly nail polish bottles side by side on the mantelpiece. They stood together, green and silver-eyed.

'They're like people from Mars,' I said. 'That's what they're like.'

'Who? Granny and Grandpa? Or your little glass bottles?'

I didn't answer that. (Not sure I knew!)

'Bye-ee,' I said, leaning down to plant a great smacker on Mum's cheek. 'Be good. And thanks for the story.'

Mum sighed.

16

'When *I* was young,' she said, 'daughters asked mums to tell them *proper* stories.'

I couldn't help grinning.

'Oh, well,' I told her. 'Things were different then, weren't they? Very different.'

Shrove Tuesday

BERLIE DOHERTY

Jenny came into the kitchen and sat on a stool watching her mother. She was making a batter for pancakes, beating milk and eggs into flour till the mixture in the jug was thick and creamy. She put a saucer on the top to let it stand for half an hour.

'You'll have to help me, Jenny,' she said, 'if you want pancakes for tea. I've got to be out at half-past six for night school. They're a nuisance, pancakes.'

'No, they're not,' said Jenny. 'They're fantastic. I wish we could have them once a week instead of once a year.'

'This time next year,' her mother sighed, 'you won't be eating any at all because you'll be worrying about your figure.'

Jenny pulled a face. 'Not me! I'd rather have pancakes than a figure any day.'

'Wait and see,' her mother smiled. 'Do these for me, will you?' She rolled a couple of oranges and a lemon across the work surface, and Jenny caught them just before they dropped off the edge. She loved working in the kitchen with her mother, just as she loved helping her dad in his woodshed. It gave them a special time together, just two of them. She always felt closer to them at times like this.

She quartered the fruits and arranged them in alternate strips of orange and yellow around a plate, then put them on the table with a tin of syrup.

'And brown sugar,' her mother said over her shoulder. 'You know your dad likes brown sugar on his pancakes.'

'How can I possibly remember that when we only have them once a year?' Jenny dipped her finger in the brown sugar and licked it. 'Mum,' she said. 'I've got something to tell you.' She waited with her back to her mother, her eyes closed.

Her mother was making a salad for the first course. She piled some wet lettuce leaves into a clean teatowel and gathered it up, shaking out the moisture over the sink. Jenny could feel the fine, cold spray from where she was standing. She bit her lip, willing her mother to stop.

'Have you put the cutlery out, Jen?'

'Mum.' Jenny came right up to her at the sink. 'I've got a boyfriend.'

Her mother half smiled to herself. 'Oh, well, that's all right,' she said, not looking up at her. 'Just so long as you don't start inviting him for pancakes too.'

'He wants me to go to the pictures with him on Friday.'

Her mother stopped shaking the lettuce and turned round to look at her. She saw a girl who was just a little smaller than herself, who had black wispy hair that was tied back in elastic bands, whose ankle socks were rumpled.

'That's out of the question,' she told her quietly.

Jenny had known that her mother would say that. All the same, she couldn't help the give-away disappointed tears that blurted up in her eyes.

19

'Why is it? Why is it?' Her voice was a plaintive wail, a little girl's voice, and she couldn't help it. She tried to steady it.

'For goodness' sake, you should know better than to ask me, even. Yesterday you were crying your eyes out because Lorraine's guinea pig had died. Today you're crying because I won't let you go waltzing off to the pictures with every lad you meet.'

'It's not every lad I meet. It's Alex Hartley and he's in my class.'

'You're not old enough.'

'I'm fourteen.' Jenny blew her nose on some kitchen paper. 'All my friends have got boyfriends.'

'So that's it.' Her mother turned back to the chopping board. She felt through a bowl of tomatoes for the firmest ones and began to slice them. The seeds and the flesh oozed out. Jenny watched her. She felt as if she hated her.

'First it's horses,' her mother said, matching her words to the rhythm of her slicing. 'Then it's roller boots, then it's some kind of fancy blouse with lace all over it, and now, for goodness' sake, it's boyfriends. Everyone else has got one first. It's always the same with you, young lady. You've got to have what everyone else has got.'

'I didn't get a horse.'

If Jenny's mother heard her she ignored it. 'Get Will and your dad, will you? Let's get this stuff eaten or I'll never get out tonight.'

The tone of her voice told Jenny that that was the end of the matter. Even so, she couldn't resist her parting shot as she went out of the kitchen.

'I could have just pretended I was going with

Lorraine. That's what she does, you know.'

Her mother put the bowl of salad on the table and went to wash her hands at the sink. She could see Jenny going across the yard to the wall and hoisting herself up on it to shout down the entry for Will to come in, and grazing her knees as she slid down it again.

'Wait till she opens the back gate instead of climbing the wall,' she said to herself. 'That's when she'll be old enough for boys.'

But, all the same, her heart went out to the girl, remembering herself at that age, and how she had longed to wear stockings instead of socks, and had stolen her own mother's lipstick to wear at a birthday party. She smiled to herself, and it was with a kind of nostalgia that she turned away. She looked round her neat kitchen, its surfaces wiped and gleaming, the jug of batter ready and waiting to be cooked for her family's tea because it was Pancake Tuesday. She didn't even like pancakes herself.

Jenny went into the shed to get her father. It smelt of sawdust and oil, and a bare light bulb swung from the ceiling. Her father was bending over a long hutch, planing the sides. He looked up sharply when she opened the door, then grinned and jerked his head to tell her to come in and close the door behind her.

'Tea's ready.'

'Aye. I'll not be long now.' He reached out for a sheet of sandpaper and folded it round a block of wood. Then he rubbed it along the edge of the hutch in a tender, careful motion. Yellow dust powdered his hands.

21

'Is it finished, Dad?' Jenny squatted down to watch him.

'It's looking grand, don't you reckon?' Her dad stepped back to show her how he'd fitted mesh across the door of the hutch, and where he'd put in hinges so it could swing backwards and forwards without catching. He bent down and felt round the inside of the hutch, frowning, seeking for splinters with his fingers. She could see how the brown muscles on his forearms bulged, and how the hairs were scattered with dust.

'I'll get the catch fastened on while she's out at class. Then it's done.'

'What d'you think she'll say?'

Her father shrugged. 'She'll say nowt. When that little rabbit's tucked inside it, she'll say nowt.' His voice was low and warm, and she remembered the late-night stories he used to whisper to her in the dark, when she and he were the only ones awake in the house.

'Has Will seen it?'

'Not unless he's spied through the cracks in the shed. Wouldn't put it past him, little devil.'

He stood up again and spat on his hands, rubbing them together to get rid of the sawdust powder.

'Not salad again, is it?'

'And pancakes.'

'Am I sick to death of salad! I'll sneak a bit into my pocket for the little rabbit's first tea, I reckon,' he chuckled. 'And I'll run up the road for some chips as soon as she's gone out.'

'Chips are bad for the heart,' Jenny reminded him. 'Anyway, you'll be able to fill up on pancakes.'

Her dad threw a blanket across the hutch and switched off the light before he opened the door. Jenny watched him ducking between the flapping teatowels on the line. It was already dark. She reached up to unpeg them and he stopped to help her.

'Dad. Does someone called Ed Hartley work on the buses with you?'

'Ed Hartley? Aye, he does. Why d'you ask?'

Jenny shrugged. 'I don't know. His Alex is in our class.' She shoved some pegs in her pockets. She couldn't help grinning at her dad.

'Oh aye! Alex Hartley, eh? Got his eye fixed on our Jen, has he?' Her dad chuckled and put his arm round her. 'Is that it?'

Jenny giggled.

'He'll have to come round and fight your dad for you, tell him. You're going to marry me, aren't you?'

Mrs Yates spent most of the meal standing by the cooker, making the pancakes. She listened to the family chattering at the table while the batter sizzled in the hot pan. Her mind was on the piece of work she was supposed to have completed for night school. When the batter was golden brown and loose enough to shake it in the pan she stepped away from the cooker.

'Watch!' she said. 'And keep your fingers crossed.'

Will and Jenny clapped as the pancake flipped round in mid-air and landed with a soft flop in the pan.

As she poured the next lot of batter in, Mrs Yates thought about her homework again, solving problems in her head. Perhaps she'd get a good mark this time.

Jenny and Will had four pancakes each. He ran straight out afterwards to play with his friends till bedtime, and Mrs Yates ran for her bus. Jenny and her dad did the washing-up between them, and as soon as he had gone out to the shed she rang her friend Lorraine.

'What did she say?' Lorraine asked.

'She said I can't.' Disappointment sobbed up inside her again. 'I hate her.'

'She'll come round in the end. Just keep asking her,' Lorraine said.

'She's not like that. If she says no, she means it. Will's been asking her and asking her for a rabbit, and she just gets madder and madder at him. She won't listen, not if she doesn't want to.'

'I thought you said he was getting a rabbit tomorrow.'

'Yes, but she doesn't know. Dad's just going to sneak it into our shed for him.'

They both started giggling. 'Get him to sneak Alex Hartley in as well.'

'I'll get him to make a hutch for him and his bike!'

After the phone call Jenny went out to talk to her dad. A bunch of late snowdrops gleamed in the dark and she bent down and picked them. She arranged them in a bowl in the kitchen, a present for her mum.

At night school Mrs Yates was doing a maths test. She did maths on Tuesdays and English on Thursdays. With a bit of luck she'd be sitting her A levels in a year or two; maybe applying for a poly course after that. She kept her dreams to herself, though. At coffee-break she went downstairs to the coffee-lounge with the others. She and one of the other women, Ann, had become good friends through these courses. They had a lot in common. She looked forward to talking to Ann as much as coming to the classes.

'What do I do this for, Ann?' she said, laughing for the first time that day. 'My brain feels like a piece of knitting that's just dropped off its needles!'

'It's all very well for those young ones,' Ann agreed, indicating a group of school-leavers who were coming to the class to re-sit their exams. 'I'm working in a shop all day, rushed off my feet, dash home to cook tea . . . '

'Pancakes, and I can't stand the things!'

'And then it's this place, and then homework before I get to bed. And my brain's fizzing like a wasp's nest all night and I can't get to sleep!'

'I know,' Mrs Yates sighed. 'But what would we be doing if we weren't here?'

'Watching telly,' her friend agreed. 'And that's enough to send anyone round the twist.'

Mrs Yates sipped at her coffee. 'I had a shock tonight,' she said. 'My daughter wants a boyfriend, and she's only fourteen.'

'You'll not stop her now,' Ann warned her. 'Not now she's interested. It would be like trying to stop the tide coming in. And if you try to stop her, she'll only hate you for it. Don't you trust her?'

The class began to move out of the coffee-bar. Clutching her books to her, Mrs Yates followed them. 'She's only a child,' she said at last. 'She's my little girl.'

Mr Yates always picked his wife up after classes. They often went for a quick drink on the way home, sometimes with people from the class. Mr Yates would just sit and smile at them and let them get on with their talking. He'd rather be down at the busmen's club, any day. When they got home that night Will was waiting on the stairs for them.

'What on earth are you doing out of bed?' Mrs Yates gasped. Her mind flew back to her earlier conversation with Jenny. 'She's not sneaked out, has she?' She had a picture of Jenny standing in a shop doorway somewhere, kissing and cuddling with some spotty lad from school.

'She's been sick,' said Will. He hunched his pyjama trousers up till the waist elastic was over his shoulders.

'It's all those pancakes,' Mrs Yates said, relieved. 'I knew it would happen.'

Jenny groaned from upstairs.

'As if I haven't had enough for today,' Mrs Yates said.

Her husband scooped Will up over his shoulder and carried him upside-down and giggling to his bed.

'And you'll have him sick, too,' she called, 'if you don't watch it.'

She went into Jenny's room.

'Did you do it down the toilet?' she asked.

'Mum, I feel awful,' Jenny moaned.

'Maybe you'll think twice before you guzzle four pancakes next time,' her mother said. 'I'll fetch you some boiled water to sip.'

She bent down and covered Jenny up with her quilt.

'My tummy hurts,' Jenny groaned.

'It will do, if you've been sick. Lie still now.'

'You don't know how much it hurts,' Jenny gasped.

Mrs Yates turned away. She knew Jenny was playing for sympathy, trying to make her feel guilty. Well, it wouldn't work. She was too old now for that kind of behaviour. She went downstairs and boiled up some water. Her kitchen gleamed in the moonlight. The snowdrops trailed out of their bowl, dead already, their white tips brown. Mrs Yates scooped them up and pushed them into the kitchen bin, and washed the bowl. Then she took the drink upstairs. Jenny was lying with her knees hunched up, groaning softly.

'Come on, it's not that bad,' her mother said.

'It is,' Jenny said. 'It's terrible.'

Her mother opened the window. 'There, that'll cool you down.' She put her hand on her daughter's forehead.

'Don't go,' Jenny whispered.

Mrs Yates hesitated for a moment. She was tired. She had to go to work in the morning. 'I'll leave the door open,' she promised. 'I'll hear you over the landing.'

She went into her own room. From there she could hear the shuddering sobs of someone beginning to cry. She's trying to make me feel guilty, she thought. I know her tricks. Her husband was asleep already, his spectacles looped over the alarm clock, ready for tomorrow to start.

Some time later Will crept into their room. He hated going into his parents' room at night. His

27

mother snored loudly and levelly. Sometimes Will would hear his father shouting at her to shut up. Sometimes, he knew, his father would creep downstairs, spectacles and alarm clock in his hand, and stretch himself out on the settee in the front room.

Will waited for a pause in the snores. 'Jenny's been sick again,' he said. He held his pyjama trousers bunched up by the waist in both his hands, because the elastic had snapped. 'She says she's got a terrible pain,' he shouted at the top of his voice.

Both his parents sat up in bed. Jenny moaned into the darkness.

'Doctor,' Mr Yates said.

'Not at this time of night,' his wife said.

'That's what they're paid for, you silly ass,' Mr Yates shouted.

Will knew it was only because he was worried.

Jenny's pain kept slipping away from her like a shiny eel and twisting back inside her again. She heard the doctor coming, and felt herself being lumped about as she was carried downstairs. She gazed up at Dad, who looked strange without his spectacles, and at Will, who was in Dad's arms, and something like a tickle in her memory reminded her that something nice was going to happen to Will soon though she couldn't remember what it was. She saw the ambulance waiting outside with its blue flashing light, and then she was being bobbed along to it with her head looking up at the stars. She climbed out of another wave of pain and knew she was speeding along in the ambulance and that Mum was there. That was all right; Mum bending towards her and holding her hand; Mum's kind round face looking worried and scared.

When the ambulance stopped she felt herself being bumped about again and wheeled into a brightly lit building with a white ceiling. There were people peering over her, large kind faces. Someone peeled off her clothes and put her into a shift that felt like a cardboard cutout. Then the walls narrowed and the pain grew as sharp as icicles that glittered and dripped with hurt, and then Mum wasn't there any more.

She lay in a kind of drowsy darkness. Something was pulling her out of it. She felt very calm, as if she were lying on her back and floating along on a dark, smooth river. But she couldn't make out the sound that was pulling her out of the water, from far away and long ago it came, then nearer and newer, a grunting, wheezing kind of sound that rose and fell, rose and fell in a deep rhythm. At last she pulled herself away from the sound and knew what it was.

'Mum,' she whispered. She couldn't believe how tiny and far away her voice was. 'Mum. You're snoring.'

Her mother jerked awake, unsure herself of where she was. She gazed round, aware of a bed near her with tubes strung above it. Day was coming cold and grey through some white shutters across the wide windows. She was sitting on a hard chair beside a hospital bed. She stood up, aching and cold, and looked down at her daughter. Jenny was as white as a doll, calm and quiet and grave, her eyelids closing, her dark hair spread round her on the pillow. She looked like a little girl again. And she looked like a young woman, serene.

'You've had your appendix out, love,' Mrs Yates said.

Jenny nodded. 'I thought so,' she whispered. Her mouth was dry.

'It's all over. It's all behind you now.'

'I feel sleepy,' Jenny murmured.

'That's right, love. You sleep properly now the anaesthetic's worn off. It'll do you good.'

Mrs Yates patted her daughter's hand.

'You've been a brave girl,' she said.

Jenny smiled.

Mrs Yates looked round at the chair. She must have slept on it for hours, waiting for Jenny to come round. She was stiff and cold. She looked back at Jenny. She wanted to pick her up and rock her in her arms as if she was a little baby again. She wanted to say she was sorry, and she didn't know how.

Jenny opened her heavy eyelids. 'You go and get some sleep, Mum.' Her voice was slurred and soft, calm and full of comfort. 'I'm all right.' She drifted off before she'd finished the last sentence. Mrs Yates knew she was right. There was nothing she could do for her now. The nurses knew what to do. Sadly she picked up her bag, gave Jenny's sleeping face a kiss, and tiptoed out of the ward.

By the time she got home her husband was getting Will ready for school.

'I'll drop him off at school and nip down to the hospital,' he told her. 'You get some kip.'

'Mummy,' said Will. 'There's something better than magic for me in the shed. Daddy's going to show it to me at lunchtime.'

'Is there?' Mrs Yates looked down at her little boy. She felt as if she'd been away from home for ages. Her head was heavy with worry and weariness.

'Bed,' her husband told her, helping her off with her coat.

Mrs Yates had something to do first. She swallowed hard.

'I don't suppose Jenny mentioned a boy to you, did she?'

Her husband laughed. 'Alex Hartley. Think there's a romance budding there.'

Mrs Yates looked out of the window. The snowdrops by the shed were a smudge of brilliance, huddled away from the wind.

'I think I'll give Lorraine a ring before school,' she said. 'She might just like to bring that lad round to see Jenny at visiting time.'

She glanced at her husband, and at Will, clean and eager for school with his new box of colouring pencils clutched in his hand.

'It won't do any harm, will it?'

And her husband touched her hand and said, 'No, love. It won't.'

The Pram Lady

VIVIEN ALCOCK

They walked in silence, partly because the hill was steep and it was hot, and partly because they had run out of things to say. They did not know each other very well. They'd only met last week at somebody's party, but already William was beginning to wonder whether he was in love.

Somehow it made conversation difficult. He wanted to impress her but his head felt hot and stupid. His mouth filled with saliva so that he had to keep swallowing, and his voice, when he did speak, sounded thick and strange. Either it was love or he was sickening for something.

The girl walked quietly by his side. Her face had lost its earlier animation, and looked sad and remote. Perhaps she was bored.

When they were halfway up the hill an extraordinary figure, wheeling a battered, old-fashioned pram, came out of a side-turning and crossed the road in front of them. She, for it was some sort of woman, was enormously fat. Her head was covered by an ancient and unravelling straw hat, around which were attached a few crumpled and faded red silk roses. From beneath the brim, streaky grey hair draggled on her shoulders. She was wearing a man's tweed jacket, liberally splattered by stains of every colour. A purple skirt, also stained, reached nearly to her bare ankles. Her large and grubby feet were in thonged sandals. The pram, as far as he could see, for she was walking away from them at a surprisingly rapid pace, was filled not with a baby but with jumble.

'God, what a fright, what a ridiculous creature,' William said, nudging the girl beside him. 'Whatever can it be?'

'It,' the girl said coldly, 'is my mother.'

He laughed, not believing her, for the woman, though he had hardly seen her face in the shadow of the straw hat, had nevertheless seemed far too old to be the mother of a sixteen-year-old girl. Nor could he believe that a girl like Helena, so beautiful, so cool and clean with her shining brown hair and her pale-green dress, could have any connection with that dreadful old bag woman.

'Some mother!' he said, grinning, and saw too late the anger and contempt in her eyes.

'I never want to see you again!' she shouted, and turning, went running down the hill.

After a stunned moment, he raced after her, caught her up, began to apologise breathlessly – what could he say? He didn't know. He could only stammer:

'I – didn't mean . . . I'm sorry . . . I didn't mean that woman, that lady – I meant – it was a dog! Didn't you see that funny dog? That's what I was talking about . . .'

But his lies were no good. 'There was no dog,' she said angrily and walked on. When he caught her by the arm, she told him to let go or she'd scream. He should have believed her because she carried out her threat, opening her mouth wide and screaming loudly. People looked over their garden walls, came out of houses, opened their windows. He was forced to let her go. She ran across the road, jumped on to a bus and was carried out of sight.

Helena Banks, having travelled the short distance home by bus and not by foot, arrived there ten minutes before her mother, and lay in wait. As soon as she heard the front door open and the squeaky bump of the pram wheels over the threshold, she ran out into the hall.

'You've done it! You've done it again!' she shouted furiously. 'I could kill you!'

'I hoped you hadn't noticed me,' her mother said sheepishly. 'I'm sorry, dear. But I thought you said you were going up to town. I thought I was safe.'

'We changed our minds.'

'I'm sorry,' her mother said again. She wheeled the pram through the hall and into her workroom at the back of the house. Helena followed her, grabbed her by the shoulders and swivelled her round, forcing her mother to confront her own reflection in the large studio mirror.

'Look at yourself! Don't you look disgusting? That horrible hat!' She snatched it off her mother's head, tried to tear it with her hands but, finding the straw tougher than it looked, threw it on the floor and stamped on it.

'I got it at the scouts' jumble sale for five pence,' her mother said wistfully. 'I thought the roses were a pretty colour. I didn't mean to wear it. I thought I might use it in a still life one day. But I couldn't find my white hat this morning. The sun was so bright, I needed something to shield my eyes. You haven't seen my white hat anywhere, have you?'

'If you mean that thing I threw in the dustbin last week,' Helena said, 'it wasn't white. It hasn't been white for years.'

Her mother sighed, took a canvas carefully out of the pram and put it on the easel by the window. It was a painting of some boys fishing in one of the Highgate ponds, bold and splashy – you could feel the sun was hot and the water wet. Helena liked her mother's paintings but would have sacrificed them all to have a more ordinary mother, one who would pass in a crowd without heads turning to stare, elbows nudging – 'God, what a fright!'

Her friends' mothers who painted didn't go around looking like bag women. They wore pretty, flowered smocks, kept their paints in neat satchels and their fingernails clean.

'Bunch of amateurs,' her mother had snorted when Helena had pointed this out.

'Mark's father is a professional and he doesn't look like a discarded paint rag tied round a pudding –'

'He does abstracts. Never has to set foot outside when he's working, so how do you know what he looks like then? He may paint in the nude, for all you know. That's one way of keeping your clothes clean. Perhaps I should try it.'

The idea of her fat mother painting in the nude had made Helena laugh. But she didn't feel like laughing now. She had liked William better than anyone else. She hadn't wanted to lose him. Ever since she had started at the sixth-form college she had made new friends only to lose them again;

sometimes in a few days, sometimes after weeks, but always sooner or later they had seen her mother wheeling her terrible pram and had laughed. 'Hey, just look at that old fright.'

And that was that. All over. The end. Helena never wanted to see them again, refused their telephone calls, tore up their letters, walked past them, stony-faced, in the corridors or in the streets outside the college.

She never warned them. Never said, as she might have done, 'My mother's a painter. She's a bit eccentric, so if you see a large woman in peculiar clothes wheeling a pram full of easels and canvases and rags through the streets of Highgate, it'll just be my mother going out to work. Don't laugh. I never forgive people who laugh at my mother. I'm the only person who's allowed to do that.'

Sometimes she felt more like crying.

She watched her mother washing her brushes at the sink in the corner of the workroom, first in white spirit and then in soap and water, carefully, paying more attention to them than she ever did to herself.

'Why don't you wash your own hair while you're about it?' Helena asked. 'It's horrible. You're not young any more. Grey hair looks awful when it's long.'

'It's not grey,' her mother protested, glancing sideways at the mirror, 'At least, not all of it. Perhaps I should have it dyed.'

'No. Have it cut short. And permed.'

'Then I'd look like every other ageing woman. But that's what you want, isn't it, Helena? An ordinary mother like your friends have. You're very conventional. It's not your fault. You take after your father. That's all he wanted, a wallpaper wife, something decorative but quiet in the background that he didn't have to listen to. It was the beginning of my real life when he walked out. I felt like cheering.'

'Will you cheer when I walk out?' Helena asked, and saw the sudden fear in her mother's eyes.

'Helena –'

But Helena left the room, slamming the door behind her.

She ran up to her bedroom and thought about packing. She could go to her father. It wasn't his day for her but that didn't matter. He and Nicole had often said, 'You know you're welcome here any time, Helena.'

She liked her father's second wife well enough, liked their neat, comfortable home. She could have gone to live with them permanently, they'd said so, but she'd always refused. She couldn't walk out and leave her mother, like Dad had done. Not that she blamed him, but if she walked out too, her mother would be alone. There'd be no one to look after her, to stop her from eating all the time; meat pies and crisps, cream doughnuts and Danish pastries, and bags of chocolate fudge wedged among the tubes of paint in her workroom, the paper smudged with blue and green and red from her fingers. No one to throw away her crazy hats when they became too dirty. No one to remind her to have her hair cut.

Helena could manage to do without boyfriends, but she did not think her mother could do without her.

When William had watched the bus carrying Helena away, he had told himself he was well out of that one. The little bitch! That awful mother! He laughed aloud, trying to convince himself – and anyone who was staring at him – that he didn't care that she'd ditched him. There were plenty more girls in the sea – and he hoped they'd all drown.

But that night he couldn't sleep for thinking about Helena. He saw again the anger and contempt in her eyes when she'd said she never wanted to see him again; and hid his face in shame, remembering how he'd nudged her in the ribs and giggled and called her poor old mother a fright. How could he have been so heartless, so vulgar? He, who prided himself on his compassion for the whole world, who ran in marathons for charity, gave ten per cent of his pocket money to Oxfam, how could he have insulted a woman just because she was poor and peculiar?

Would Helena ever forgive him? She must, she must, he thought, turning and tossing on his moonlit bed. He'd apologise tomorrow at college. He'd take her flowers from the garden.

But Helena would not listen to his apologies. She threw his flowers on the floor and ran off. When he cornered her by the library, she put her fingers in her ears and threatened to scream again if he didn't go away. He did not doubt that she would. She was amazing. He'd never met a girl like her before. But then he'd never been in love.

He was a stubborn boy. He refused to give up. He wrote her letters at college but she tore them up and sent them back to him. He followed her home and she threatened to call a policeman and complain that he was molesting her.

'I'm not. I just want to say I'm sorry.'

'All right, you've said it. Now go away.'

'Will you forgive me?'

'No.'

'I'll never stop saying sorry until you do.'

'God, what a bore you are!' she shouted, and ran into the house, slamming the door in his face when he tried to follow. Looking out of the net curtains in the living room, she saw him standing gazing up at the house. She thought he looked surprised. Had he expected them to live in cardboard boxes? Probably. He'd obviously taken her mother for a tramp.

'Isn't that the boy I saw you with last week?' her mother asked, joining her at the window.

'Yes.'

'He looks nice.'

'He's a pest. He won't leave me alone.'

'You're lucky,' her mother said. 'I wouldn't want a boy like that to leave me alone, if I was your age.'

'I hate him,' Helena said. She flung open the window at the bottom and shouted it aloud. 'Go away! I hate you! I hate you!'

William looked at her sadly for a moment, then he turned and walked off.

'Now you've driven him away,' her mother said. 'Poor young man. He looked so nice. I hope you don't come to regret it.'

'You wouldn't think he was so nice if you knew what he'd said about you.'

'What was that?'

Helena told her.

'I don't suppose he knew I was your mother,' Mrs

Banks said generously. 'You oughtn't to hold it against him. You've called me worse things than that and I've always forgiven you.'

'That's different. I'm your daughter,' said Helena, and then added slowly, 'besides, I understand. I know why you've let yourself go like this. It's because of Dad, isn't it? You don't care what you look like any more since Dad left. You've given up.'

'Oh, Helena!' Mrs Banks said, half laughing, half ashamed. 'You've forgotten. I've always been fat and untidy. Don't you remember how it got on your poor father's nerves? I expect that was partly why we broke up. We just weren't suited. He was always so neat and so particular, and as for me – ' She walked over to the mirror and regarded her reflection critically. 'You know, I really don't care what I look like, but it's not fair on you, is it? Or on the unfortunate young men who laugh at me, not knowing I'm your mother. Why don't you laugh with them, Helena? I won't mind.' She smiled. 'My shoulders are broad enough.'

'I can't,' Helena said. 'I hate it. I won't have them laughing at you.'

Her mother looked at her. 'I'll start dieting tomorrow,' she promised. 'It'll be good for me. And I'll have my hair cut and curled. Poor Helena, I'll do my best not to shame you in front of your next boyfriend.'

'It doesn't matter,' Helena said. 'I don't want any more boyfriends.'

Her mother raised her eyebrows thoughtfully, but did not say anything.

Helena did not see William again that term. He was

not at college the next day or for the rest of the week before they broke up for the holidays. She'd have liked to have asked his friends where he was, but she was afraid they'd tell him. She wished her mother would ask about him, if only to hear his name again, but her mother was busy painting, making use of the long, light evenings to get ready for an exhibition.

Oddly, now that William was gone, Helena was haunted by him. She seemed to see him everywhere out of the corner of her eyes, but when she looked round, he was not there. Her mind was filled with images of him. Sometimes she seemed to hear his voice. She began to dream of him at night, dreams dominated by the tall, thin, unhappy figure. Sometimes he was in a street market, sometimes walking down a shabby street, once he crouched in an empty field with his hands over his eyes — but always there was a sense of bleak misery about him that made her wake up shivering. She began to wonder if he was dead.

At last she could bear it no longer. She went into her mother's workroom and said, 'Mum, do you remember William Rendell? The boy I shouted at? The one you said looked nice?'

'Yes, I do. I remember him well.'

'I'm a bit worried about him. He wasn't at college for the last week and I haven't seen him anywhere. I wondered if he was ill.'

Her mother didn't say anything. She was looking at her painting, her eyes narrowed. Helena glanced at it. Her mother had painted a group of cyclists on what appeared to be a large, otherwise empty concrete playground. The bicycle wheels, set at different angles, made an abstract pattern, echoed and somehow made sinister by the distorted shadows on the concrete. On the left side there was a solitary cyclist, a tall, thin youth with drooping shoulders, who watched the others with the sad air of an outcast.

'That looks a bit like William,' Helena said.

Her mother did not answer. Helena, glancing quickly at her, caught the tail of a disappearing smile on her face. She stared back at the painting, and then at the completed canvases hanging on the walls on the workroom. They were all figure compositions; people in street markets, sitting in trains, walking along deserted roads, standing waiting on windy railway platforms – and in every one, sometimes in the foreground, sometimes half hidden in a corner, was the figure of a dejected youth, thin and tall, with untidy dark hair and sad eyes. William Rendell.

'He came to see me one day when you were at college,' her mother said. 'Such a nice boy. He brought me some red roses and told me what had happened, how you'd quarrelled because he'd been rude about me. He was very upset, very ashamed of himself, poor boy, and really, as I told him, it wasn't his fault. It was mine for going about looking such a guy. I have been dieting, Helena. I've already lost six pounds – not that it shows yet, a mere drop in the ocean. William offered to sit for me for nothing, to make amends, he said. I think he really hoped to see you. However, I'm not one to turn my nose up at a free model. He was very useful.' She waved her hands at the paintings on the wall. 'Very patient. I'm doing a portrait of him for his mother.'

She took the cyclists off the easel and put another canvas in its place.

'What do you think of that?' she asked.

The painted William sprawled on the studio chair. His glossy eyes looked straight out of the canvas into hers. His painted mouth turned up in a hopeful smile. He did not look sad any more. He looked pleased with himself, like a cat who's found a comfortable home at last and hopes it will be allowed to stay.

'He's coming for the last sitting this afternoon,' her mother said. 'He should be here any minute. I suppose you wouldn't stay in and make us all tea, would you, darling?'

It had been a plot, Helena thought, looking round at all the painted Williams. She'd been brainwashed. They'd been in it together, William and her mother, that was obvious. But she couldn't help laughing.

'Oh, all right,' she said. 'I'll make tea for you both. But you're not to have any cake. Me and William will eat it all.'

Forbidden Clothes

JAMILA GAVIN

'They are taking her away from us.'

Mrs Khan articulated her words in a flat, mono-tone voice but, as she spoke, she leaned forward and stared intensely into the eyes of her volunteer English teacher, Margot Henderson.

Margot stared back, momentarily shocked out of her boredom. This was the first English sentence Mrs Khan had put together herself after nearly six weeks of lessons.

'What do you mean?' asked Margot.

Still leaning forward, Mrs Khan spoke again. She repeated the same sentence, hammering it out with staccato precision.

'They are taking her away from us.'

'Who is taking who away from you?' asked Margot, looking round.

Then she met the large, dark eyes of the fifteen-year-old girl in the school photograph. It sat alone on the mantelpiece, testifying to the reverence and devotion accorded to an only child.

She wasn't beautiful. Her face had been left to fend for itself, framed only by a severe headscarf which swept her hair away out of sight. Her nose was too long and narrow, her cheekbones too angular, her mouth too broad. Yet there was something compelling about the way she looked almost defiantly into the camera, as if she was trying to say, 'Yes, this is me. There's more to me than meets the eye.'

'Nasreen.' Mrs Khan whispered her daughter's name.

'Ah, yes! Nasreen!' repeated Margot, brightly. 'How is she getting on at school?' Margot asked her question loudly and slowly as if the woman were deaf.

Mrs Khan opened her mouth and drew in her breath sharply as she struggled to find the words.

'She . . . she . . . not . . . fine. Fine . . .' She shrugged helplessly and slumped back in her seat, drawing her veil across her face.

Margot felt the irritation rising up in her. Mrs Khan was not her favourite pupil. She was a slow learner, and she resented the sense of dumb depression which seemed to envelop the woman, slowing down her movements and imprinting an expression of wooden despair on her face.

'Don't just say "fine", Mrs Khan. Put it in a sentence,' urged Margot with exaggerated patience. 'Nasreen is fine.'

'No!' exclaimed Mrs Khan sharply. 'Nasreen is . . . no . . . fine . . .' she struggled desperately.

'You mean, Nasreen is *not* fine,' corrected Margot.

'Nasreen is *not* fine,' repeated Mrs Khan obediently.

'Is something wrong at school?' asked Margot. She glanced at her watch and noted with relief that their time was up.

Mrs Khan saw the movement. She stood up, twisting the ends of her veil in her fingers.

'Yes, it is time for me to go,' said Margot, thankfully. She was really not in the mood for trying to extricate sufficient English out of Mrs Khan to find out what was bothering her.

'If you have a problem with Nasreen, the best thing to do is talk to the school,' said Margot. 'Perhaps your husband can. He speaks good English, doesn't he?' Then, giving her a kindly pat on the arm, she gathered up her text book.

'Try and work through the exercises we have covered today, OK? and I'll see you next week.' Then she made her own way to the front door and opened it.

'Goodbye, Mrs Khan.'

Mrs Khan didn't reply, but stood in the semi-darkness at the rear of the hall. She looked as if she were being swallowed up within her satin tunic and pyjamas, as she clutched the veil around herself.

'By-ee!' repeated Margot, giving a cheery wave, and shut the front door behind her.

'Nasreen! Nasreen! Come on, we'll miss the bus!' Louise Dibben danced impatiently at her friend's elbow, as she stood in front of the long mirror, fluffing out her hair and squirting clouds of hair lacquer into it.

'How do I look?' asked Nasreen, twisting her head to examine her profile.

'You look great, really great! Now come on. If we miss the bus it will all be for nothing.'

'OK, I'm coming.' She gave a last critical glance at herself. The transformation was pretty good. From her demure, sexless school uniform with headscarf and slacks for modesty, she had squeezed herself into a tight elasticated pair of jeans for which she had secretly saved up for weeks to buy. They flattered her figure, she thought, emphasising her long legs and narrow waist.

'Does my bum look too big?' she asked, turning sideways.

'You look great, I tell you,' insisted Louise, 'and I like your top an' all,' she added. 'You got better boobs than me, lucky thing. But hurry up.'

'We're all right for time,' said Nasreen, glancing at her watch. 'Stop panicking! We've got five minutes yet. I've got to do me eyes.'

Louise sighed and sat on her bed. 'God! If your mum and dad could see you now they'd have a blooming fit.'

'My dad would kill me,' murmured Nasreen, as she brushed the mascara on to her eyelashes.

Nasreen had taken to coming back to Louise's house most days after school. Gradually she had built up a secret wardrobe of leggies and low-cut tops, of miniskirts and T-shirts, sometimes plain and some-times with slogans brazened across her chest.

'My forbidden clothes,' she would laugh. She felt like Cinderella transforming herself to go out and have a ball, then rushing back to change into her uniform, headscarf and dull slacks, so that when she went back home she would once more be the demure, innocent little girl her parents thought she was.

Nasreen still shuddered when she remembered the pain of those early days at Merton Close. She had never been made to feel different before. But now all people seemed to see were her differences: her different coloured skin, her different clothes, her different voice and, most of all, her different religion. She was nothing but a Paki, until Louise decided to be her friend.

Louise was brash, Louise was loud, Louise was a leader. People listened to her. She seemed so grown-up. She was the first to perm her hair and wear tight, short skirts; she was the first to have a boyfriend and sit smoking in the bus shelter with him. She had opinions, and talked back to teachers, so Nasreen was astonished when, one day, Louise marched up to her with a maths book and said, 'Hey, Nasreen! You're good at maths. Help me with this.'

They began going to each other's houses, but Nasreen knew her mother didn't like Louise and thought she was a bad influence so, instead, she only went round to Louise's house.

Nasreen loved the Dibben household. It was so different from her own clean, silent, scrupulously tidy home. Here it looked as if a tornado had struck it most of the time: always buried under a rubble of toys and washing, of babies' bottles and half-chewed rusks. Yet it was a good-natured chaos, and no one minded if she and Louise slumped across the sofa watching television and munching sandwiches.

'Wanna go with me to the disco?' Louise asked her one day.

'Oh, no! I couldn't!' Nasreen looked shocked at the prospect, then disappointed because she wished she could go. 'I'd never be allowed,' she said, sadly.

'Don't tell 'em then,' snapped Louise, bold as brass.

'Anyway, I've got no clothes,' added Nasreen. 'I couldn't go like this!'

'Borrow mine,' retorted Louise. Then she shrieked excitedly. 'Hey! Let me dress you up! Please, Nasreen! Just for fun!'

So that's how it all started.

'There! OK?' She turned round to show her friend her face with her painted eyelids, stiff, blackened lashes, the hint of blusher on her cheeks and just the right shade of lipstick to tone in.

'Beautiful!' exclaimed Louise, generously. 'Now let's go!'

The two girls clattered downstairs.

An admiring whistle rang out from the kitchen. Louise's younger brother, Craig, gave a cheeky wave. 'Like your jeans, Nasreen! Sexeee!'

'Oh shut up!' squealed Nasreen, but she was pleased.

Sitting at the back of the bus, Nasreen and Louise admired each other and laughed at the world they had set out to conquer. In ten minutes they had alighted in the centre of town and made their way along to the precinct where they knew all their friends would be congregating.

'Carl's there,' Louise hissed at her friend.

'So?' exclaimed Nasreen, flushing.

'You know you want to get off with him, and he's just split up with Denise.'

'Has he?' cried Nasreen. 'Why didn't you tell me before? Oh God, how do I look?'

'I've told you. You look fabulous. If he doesn't fall for you, he's a blind dope. Oh good, there's Mark,' Louise squealed, and ran over to join her boyfriend.

★ ★ ★

49

The telephone rang. 'It's me . . .'

'Where are you?' wailed Mrs Khan. 'Why weren't you on the bus?'

'Mum, I went back to Louise's house. We're doing our homework together. She's miles better at geography than me, and she's helping me,' explained Nasreen, convincingly.

'But what about tea?' asked Mrs Khan. 'I've got yours all ready here.'

'Sorry, Mum,' said Nasreen. 'Louise's mum gave me some, so I'm fine. Must go. We've got tons to get done.'

'When will you be home?' asked Mrs Khan quickly, trying to hang on to her daughter's voice.

'Well . . .' Nasreen answered vaguely. 'I think we've got another hour or two's work, because after geography, I said I'd help Louise with her maths. I'm better at that than her. OK?'

Mrs Khan hesitated, trying desperately to assert her authority.

'Get back before your dad does, won't you?'

'Of course I will, Mum. Must go. Bye!' And the phone went dead.

'OK?' asked Carl as she came out of the phone booth.

'Yeh!' Nasreen smiled sweetly at him, and slipped her arm in his.

'Have we time to go to the Flamingo? Have a quick drink?' asked Carl. 'Louise and Mark have gone on ahead.'

'Of course!' cried Nasreen, happily. 'But I've got to be changed and on that eight o'clock bus home. Me dad gets in at nine, and I've got to make it before he does, or else there'll be hell to pay.'

★ ★ ★

Mrs Khan stood in the bay window. Although darkness had fallen, she hadn't put on the light, but had drawn aside the net curtains to gaze, invisibly, up and down the empty street outside.

A hard lump of anxiety pressed into her chest so that it hurt to breathe. She was afraid, but then she realised she had always been afraid. Ever since Nasreen had moved up into secondary school, things had changed.

They used to walk together, side by side, friends; but then Nasreen took to going on ahead or dawdling behind her mother. Even the way she walked changed. Instead of the leisurely, shy walk, she now strode, long-legged, looking more and more like a western girl despite her headscarf and the slacks under her school uniform. On approaching the school gates she would suddenly see her friends and, tossing out the word 'goodbye' as if to no one in particular, she would disappear into the school, arms linked and immersed in the sound of gossip and laughter. She never looked back these days.

That was when the lump of misery took residence in Mrs Khan's heart.

'They are taking her away . . . taking her away . . .' She hissed the words out in English, as if someone would hear and understand her fears.

She felt a sudden surge of anger as she remembered her English teacher.

'They? Who's they?' Mrs Khan could hear the indifferent voice as Margot Henderson asked the question.

'They? Why the Dibbens of course!' Mrs Khan answered it now to the empty room, spotlessly clean, neat and devoid of any signs of human activity – just as Mr Khan liked to have it when he came home.

The Dibbens. Mrs Khan clasped her arms tightly around her body, straitjacketing herself, as if afraid if she did not she might scream at the world: 'I'm lonely! I'm lonely! And they're taking my child away from me.'

'Nasreen?' The sound of the front door sent her scurrying to the hall. Nasreen tossed her schoolbag inside, and kicked the front door closed.

'Hi, Mum!' she said indifferently, and did not look her in the eye. 'Sorry I'm late, we had tons of homework. I'm going to my room. I'm tired and I just want to flop!'

'Nasreen!' Mrs Khan reached out and touched her daughter's cheek. She wanted to clasp her, reclaim her. 'Did you have supper?' she asked. 'I made your favourite pakoras. Come to the kitchen and have some.'

'No, Mum!' Nasreen refused impatiently. 'I'm not hungry. I had plenty to eat at Louise's. Just let me go to my room,' and she shook herself free from her mother's grasp and rushed upstairs.

Once in her room, she hastily removed the rest of her forbidden clothes. She carefully folded them into a carrier bag and tucked it right at the back of her wardrobe.

Then she sat in front of her mirror. Had her mother noticed remnants of make-up? She leaned forward to scrutinise herself and looked into her own eyes. They were still shining with excitement.

Carl had seen her home. Carefully, of course, because it wouldn't do for any of the neighbours to see her – especially anyone from her own community. They had hidden in a bus shelter while she took off her jeans and put back her school slacks under her uniform.

'What about the headscarf?' he asked, after she had shaken out her hair and re-plaited it. But she dropped her head with embarrassment. 'Oh that doesn't matter,' she said.

Of course, it did, and when he said 'goodbye' to her at the corner – he kissed her till she felt she would faint – and hurriedly walked away, she tied on her headscarf when he was out of sight and went home slowly, giving time for her flushed cheeks to calm down.

Now, as she stared at her reflection, she felt guilty. She didn't like feeling guilty; it made her angry. She didn't want to think about the shock and disappointment her father would feel if he knew what she was doing; she didn't want to think of how she was hurting her mother. At the moment, it was her mother, above all, who made her angry. She was so pliable, so pathetically vulnerable; her whole life was devoted to serving. Serving her husband; serving her daughter. Nothing she did was for her own benefit. She allowed herself to be a victim.

'I won't be like that! I won't, I won't!' Nasreen swore to herself.

Suddenly, Nasreen heard the front door. She heard her mother's puzzled footsteps hurry into the hall.

'Nasreen! Nasreen!' It was her father's voice, rough with anger.

'Nasreen's up in her room,' she heard her

mother say nervously. 'You're back early. Is everything all right?'

He ignored her and called again. 'Nasreen! Get down here! I wish to speak to you.' Fiercely he switched on all the lights.

Nasreen slowly descended the stairs, pausing halfway down, her pale face looming over the bannister.

'Hi, Dad!' She tried to sound unconcerned.

'Get down here.' He prodded his finger into the air space before him.

She continued her descent, meeting her mother's puzzled eyes at the bottom. Then she faced her father.

'Here!' He prodded the air in front of him.

'Nasreen!' Mrs Khan touched her daughter's arm. She had never seen Mr Khan look so angry. Mrs Khan wanted to protect her. She clung to her arm, pulling her back.

'What is it, Rashid? What has she done? Please don't harm her!'

'Let go of her!' His voice was cold and determined. 'Nasreen has shamed me and her family and her community, and she must be made to realise what she has done.'

'How?' cried Mrs Khan. 'What has she done? Nasreen?' She turned pitifully to her daughter. 'What have you done?'

'She has been seen in the town without her veil and slacks, dressed like one of those loose English girls, wearing a tight miniskirt, high heels and made up like a prostitute. How dare you! How dare you do this to us.' He began to remove his leather belt.

'No, Rashid, no!' begged Mrs Khan. 'I'm sure Nasreen won't do this again, will you, Nasreen?'

'And it's not the first time.' Mr Khan's voice choked with emotion. 'I now hear that this has been going on for months. Everyone in the community knows about it. Everyone has been talking about it behind our backs. You have ridiculed me!'

'Nasreen!' She looked at her daughter for some sign of repentance. But to her amazement Nasreen stood before her father, upright and unflinching as he raised his arm, moved round her, and brought the belt down across her back.

'Why are you doing this, Nasreen?' the head of her school pleaded with her.

'Why do you go on behaving in a way which upsets your mother and father and your whole community. All you get is a beating. Is it really worth it?'

Usually, Nasreen took her beatings and remonstrations sullenly, and without a word, but this time she looked up at her head teacher and said quietly, 'Sir, I'll be sixteen in two months' time. That's all the time I have left to be free. When I'm sixteen, they'll marry me off; I expect it'll be to some bloke from Pakistan who I've never met. I'm clever enough to go to university, aren't I? But I won't be allowed. I'll have to stay at home and have babies and be nothing but a good little housewife, sewing and ironing and having a meal ready in the evening. That's how it'll be when I'm sixteen. That's how it'll be for the rest of my life. Well, sir, I've got two months left, and I don't care how often I get beaten, I'm going to go into town, and dress as

I like, and smoke in shop doorways, and my dad'll have to kill me before he stops me having what freedom is left.'

'Did you ever find out what that Mrs Khan meant when she said, "They are taking her away from me?"' asked the colleague.

She and Margot Henderson had met again in the precinct coffee shop.

'Funny you should ask,' said Margot, putting down her coffee cup. 'After I last saw you, I got a message to say that Mrs Khan wanted to give up the lessons. Can't say I was disappointed. The last I heard was that the daughter, Nasreen, had run away and gone to live with her best friend.'

'What are you doing?' Louise woke and stared into the darkness. 'It's the middle of the night. Are you ill?'

She could just make out Nasreen, standing in the centre of the bedroom.

'Nasreen!' She sat up in bed and switched on her table lamp. 'What are you doing? Where are you going?'

Nasreen was fully dressed, but in her tunic, pyjamas and veil. By her side was a suitcase. She picked it up and moved towards the bedroom door.

'That's it for me now, Louise,' she said quietly. 'It's my birthday tomorrow.'

'Yeh! I know. Me and the gang, we've all got a smashing party organised for you,' cried Louise.

'Well, you'll have to have it without me,' said Nasreen. 'I'm going home. Don't try and stop me.

Please – ' She put out a resisting hand, as Louise flung her legs out of bed and made to hold her back.

'Just let me go. I know what I'm doing. I've had my fun, but it had to end. I made a pact with myself that when I'm sixteen I return to my community. It's where I really belong. Don't make it hard for me, Louise. Please. Thank you for everything you've done for me. Thank your parents, too. I'll make it up to you one day. Promise. Meantime, just let me go without any fuss.'

Then she slipped out of the door and was gone.

It wasn't quite dawn, yet Mrs Khan woke to see a rosy glow through the bedroom window. She had barely slept all night long, as she had barely slept since Nasreen left home. Now, with a dull curiosity, she slid out of bed without disturbing her sleeping husband, and went to the window.

'Rashid!' she called out uncontrollably.

He awoke instantly, alerted by the urgency in her voice. He went to her side and looked out of the window.

Nasreen had lit a bonfire. The flames shot upwards into the night sky. They could see her figure silhouetted against the firelight as from time to time she bent down and, taking a garment from the open suitcase, tossed it on to the fire. Sparks flew upwards, scattering like fireflies.

When she had emptied the suitcase, she stood transfixed for a while, staring into the embers, then, pulling her veil over her head and drawing it tightly round her shoulders, she turned towards the house.

JAMILA GAVIN

'Nasreen! Nasreen!' whispered her mother. 'At last! You have come back to us!'

Kelly

MARJORIE DARKE

My mother chose the name. Crazy, because she is usually good at thinking ahead. Nothing left to chance. If I explain that I'm a well-padded sixteen with a backside that wobbles as I walk, no matter how I try to stiffen my glutaeus maxima (bum muscles in case your human anatomy is rusty), you will see my problem.

Nicknames?

Well, there's Jellybaby. Sometimes Jellybelly when anyone really wants to take the micky . . . but I shan't go on. Make a list of everything rhyming with Kelly to get the picture.

Once I asked her what had made her pick such a weird label for a defenceless baby.

'It's a good name!' She sounded mildly surprised. 'Dad agrees. There's something stylish about the sound.'

'D'you really think so?' I smiled, briefly charmed.

'Yes, I do! Besides, Kelly was your great-granny's maiden name and I like to think of us holding hands with the past.'

The charm dwindled. I resented that 'us'. Seems to me that the present – shall I, shan't I go into the sixth form next year; job prospects; thinning ozone layer – is enough to handle without rooting through things long gone. But I wasn't going to argue. Give her any encouragement and Mum will pin back your ears for hours, rabbiting on about family history. Sometimes we seem to be living in different worlds. Mum's is an old-fashioned place where coach travel means four horses and no pneumatic tyres. She's really into uncovering our family tree. Been at it for *years*. Not in the normal way – father to grandfather to great-grandfather all helpfully sharing the same surname – but through the mothers.

'Far more logical when you think about it.' She finished the patch on my jeans and flowed to our home computer, calling up the household accounts, talking and tapping: 'Who carries the child for nine months – weightlifting twenty-four hours a day – then goes through the athletics of birth? After all, developing babies are *attached* to their mothers!'

'Umbilical cord rules OK!' David said. Picking up his soccer boots, he slung them round his skinny little neck and walked out while we were still staring.

Mum burst into such an April shower of laughs she had to mop her cheeks with several of the tissues she has ready for emergencies.

That was weeks ago. Long before Easter and the school trip to France. Almost the end of term, and on this Monday morning as I staggered from bed, family trees and umbilical cords couldn't have been further from my mind. One glance out of the window showed the sun had given up the unequal struggle. Grey everywhere. I felt pretty grey myself, catching a vision of ample fleshy chunks in the mirror as I stripped off my pyjamas. To cap everything, a large yellow pimple had swelled overnight on my nose. Sure sign my period would start in time for the Channel crossing.

'Oh, *knickers!*'

I leaned forward for closer inspection. Easter in Paris with the sun shining on the Champs Elysées, the Eiffel Tower, the shimmering Seine, Marilyn's smooth brown skin and slinky curves, Tom Hawtree (whom we both fancy) and my ripe crop of spots!

That's when David slid into my room without so much as a knock.

'Cor! Aren't you fat!' His flat stomach ballooned. His cheeks puffed. 'You shouldn't stuff yourself with crisps and Mars bars.'

It's difficult to stay calm and dignified when you're starkers. 'Get out, you little tick ... and that's *mine*,' seeing him nick the newest ballpoint from my desk. 'Put it back!'

All he did was grin in that infuriating, sleepy way he has. I could have murdered him. Instead I slung the nearest thing as he slithered through to the landing. My hairbrush hit the door, of course, ricocheted and sent my green glass frog flying from the bookshelf to the floor where it broke in three pieces, the leg bit hopping into the jumble of clothes I'd heaved into an open suitcase.

I don't know how long I stood there. My dear frog! Present from Mum after another family-tree-hunting trip. Tears pressed the back of my throat. She'd been like a gleeful little kid at discovering another Great-Great, a miner's widow this time. An enterprising old bird who'd fed her starving family by catching and cooking frogs. How Mum unearths these titbits I don't know. Though she does have a knack of persuading the most unlikely people to dredge up all sorts of tales from the murk of ages. A stubborn light comes into her eyes. Nothing can divert her. She really will approach *anybody*! It's so embarrassing.

'Quarter to eight, Kelly,' Mum called briskly up the stairs. 'Move yourself or you'll be late.' Feet followed voice.

In a panic I threw the two visible bits of glass into my suitcase. Stuffed a sweater on top. Cut myself in the process. Bled on the pants I was dragging over my elephant feet, then on the clean shirt.

'Oh, *knickers*!'

Just in time I pulled on a concealing cardigan and seized a skirt as she leaned through the doorway.

'You aren't wearing *that* to school, surely?' She eyed the skirt.

'What's wrong with it?' But I knew. Black. Ankle length. Tasselled fringe round the hem. 'Fashion freaky,' to coin her phrase.

She glanced up from the hem, the wrestling match with herself not to be over-critical turning to motherly concern. 'Oh, what a nasty boil. I'll fetch you the Zitnip.'

'I don't want the Zitnip,' I growled, big toe catching the fringe.

'Nonsense! We don't want the infection to spread.'

That maddening plural again . . . *and* my bloody toenail had split, properly hooking the fringe.

She squatted down to unravel me. Even at this early hour her hair was brushed into good behaviour. Not a fatty bulge to be seen under her well-pressed skirt and neat sweater.

Hand-wrenching, toe-tugging, I tore the fringe and almost succeeded in kicking her – resentment swelling more painfully than any zit. 'For Chrissake don't fuss, Mum. I'm not a baby. I can dress myself.'

She got up. Stalked out. And was back in time to catch me giving my nose a prod.

'Leave it, Kelly! You'll only make it worse. Do you want a permanent scar?'

'It's my bloody nose!'

Her mouth tightened and she shot me one of those disappointed looks, far more devastating than anger. 'Did anyone ever tell you that swearing is the last resort of a barren vocabulary?' Ice in her voice. The jar of Zitnip dropped on my desk with a little slam. The door slammed as well.

The zit bust anyway. Accidentally, because I couldn't keep from crying and buried my face in the pillow to stifle the racket. Afterwards, grudging shame rose from the sludge of resentment. Typical me. 'Storm in a teacup,' as Mum would say. Yet I *had* wanted to kick her. Sometimes I frighten myself.'

The bedside clock said ten past eight. No time for breakfast. I washed, showed my teeth to the toothbrush. Dabbed Zitnip on my nose. Found a plaster for my cut thumb. Hurtled down to the kitchen where a Glen Miller oldie leaked from the radio, and Marge Gifford from next door was gabbing on about something I hadn't time to tune into. I caught:

'Sheer luck,' and, 'What about this afternoon?'

'*Mu-um?*' time was galloping. 'Where's . . .'

'Usual place – work-top.'

'But it's not . . .' but it was – nestling under a pac-a-mac. 'I don't need this.'

She broke off from talking to Marge. 'Take it. The weather forecast says storms.'

Biting back my views on weather forecasts, I left the mac and, stuffing lunchbox into bag, rushed out.

More bleats from Mum: 'Kelly, have a drink of milk at least. You can't work on an empty stomach . . . Kelly, have you got your . . .'

I shut the front door, taking my frustrations with me.

The day limped on, bringing a blistering from Mrs Greatorex for not handing in the history essay, a calamity in Chemistry when I broke two test tubes, and a call to go to the office before lunch.

'Keys!' Our school secretary held them out. 'And your mother left a message to say don't worry if she's late home. Your brother will be late too, as he's going home with Sprout?' She made a question mark with her eyebrows and dropped the keys into my hand. 'Overslept, did we? And no breakfast . . . tut tut!'

Disgruntled, I hotfooted it to the hall where we eat our lunches, meeting Marilyn in the courtyard outside. She'd got her dark hair held back by a scarlet butterfly clip and looked breathtaking.

'Fuss, fuss, that's all my mum ever does,' I grumbled. 'Treats me like a baby. D'you know . . .'

'Kelly.' Marilyn's large brown eyes, always expressive, looked at me with arctic chill. 'Why don't you shut up about your mum?'

'You wouldn't say that if you were on the receiving end.'

'I should be so lucky.'

'What's that supposed to mean?'

She shrugged and swung away, long legs striding towards the playing fields before I could call and ask wasn't she coming for lunch? It was so unlike her to be moody that I worried all through my ham sarnis and yoghurt . . . until Tom Hawtree came in late and sat in the empty chair beside me.

'There's a meeting in the gym after lunch about the French trip - did you know?'

I shook my head. He'd stuffed his mouth with bread and cheese and looked rather like an endearing hamster. He glanced at his watch.

'In six minutes pre . . .cisely, Nelly. So eat up! You know how old Taylor goes berserk if people aren't punctual. We need to put a spurt on.'

I loved the plural. Temporarily Marilyn left my mind. She came back to me only when Mr Taylor counted heads. I offered to fetch her.

He twisted the end of an eyebrow. 'Exercise your memory cells, Kelly. Pass on the information later.'

So I did – on the way home in the pouring rain, finishing: 'Where were you? You had me skating all over.'

'Went for a walk. No point in bothering about that meeting. I'm not going to France after all.'

The news fell like a block of concrete, crushing the prospective fun to pulp. France without Marilyn? We'd been friends forever. Even the thought I might have a grain of a chance with Tom Hawtree was no consolation.

'Why not?'

'Other things to do.' She studied the rain bouncing back from the ground in a thousand little fountains.

'Like what, for instance?'

She didn't speak for several strides. 'I can't leave Dad on his own.' A flat, bald statement.

Unbelievable! 'You make him sound a proper wet wally. What about your mum?'

We had reached the road where we separate to go to our homes. She stopped abruptly, turning on me, words fairly spitting out.

'Shut your mouth! You don't know *anything*.' Her cheeks were running with water, not all of it rain.

I put a hand on her arm. 'Marilyn, what's wrong?'

She shrugged me off. 'If you must know, *she* walked out on us yesterday. Now why don't you push off. Your mummy will be waiting with a nice hot drink.' She began to run away.

I wanted to sprint after her. Say how sorry I was. Hug her. But what chance had my short fat legs against her athletic beauties! I did call: 'Come back with me!' But if she heard, she didn't let on.

I opened the front door into peace and warmth, still reeling under Marilyn's bombshell, wondering how she felt stepping into emptiness – a house without a heart.

Upstairs in our cosy bathroom I stripped, turned on the taps and went to my bedroom to collect dry clothes, still so absorbed in thinking about her it took a moment before my brain translated what my eyes saw.

The suitcase was shut and fastened!

I hadn't given the broken frog a thought since Marilyn's huff at lunchtime.

Opening the lid, I found the rubble of clothes resolved into neat folds. No glass. But there were foreigners – underwear, washing kit, socks and tights rolled into neat balls, that *pac-a-mac*! I looked at it with hatred. Strange how such an insignificant thing can suddenly represent everything that has bugged you for years.

I emptied the lot on the floor. Took what was necessary. Stormed back to the bath and lay there muttering horrible threats at the sponge and the pumice stone.

But fury can't compete against the lap of hot water and steam rising with scents of Aloe Vera from melted bath beads. Gradually I relaxed. Down below the front door opened. I recognised the clicks and pauses, the weight of footsteps on the carpet. Mum called:

'That you, Kelly?' Her usual remark.

'No, it's the milkman.' My usual answer.

'Cream and two yoghourt then.'

A well-rehearsed little play – silly and comfortable.

Lazing in the slosh of water I heard David come back, and the kitchen clatterings as Mum prepared our tea. Poor Marilyn – she'd have to cook for herself, unless her dad knew how. Our dad couldn't so much as boil an egg! No need with Mum around. But if ever she wasn't . . .?

I got out, dried and dressed, then repacked the suitcase before going downstairs – choosing the living room rather than the kitchen and possible froggy conversation. I was still there, wrestling with the history essay and trying to resist half a bag of crisps I'd discovered lurking at the bottom of my bag, when David burst in.

'The chip pan's on fire!'

'Yeah, yeah – a space ship's hovering over our back garden.'

'No kidding,' he squeaked. 'Mum's gone next door.'

I sniffed, sprang up showering crisps and belted down our hall, still not believing my nose. Mum would never leave the gas burning? Greasy acrid mist drifted towards me. On the cooker the pan had a sort of flambeau. I looked frantically for something to smother the flames. Nothing but a bloody oven glove! I slipped it on. The handle seemed okay, so I risked carrying the blaze into the yard and put it down – Mum strolling up the path, carton in hand, casual . . . then haring towards our watering-can.

I yelled: 'NO!' too late . . . and ran at her, crashing us against the wall. As we fell in a heap, water hit burning oil with an explosion of flame that roared skywards, hung, then died into bitter black smoke.

Trembling, we picked ourselves up from a wreckage of eggs.

'They were for supper.' Her voice shook. 'Egg and chips, your favourite. To cheer you up . . . but I forgot to go to the supermarket. I was borrowing from Marge . . . you know how she goes on.' She spread her hands, looking at the dirt and egg in disbelief. Stunned.

'Tea,' I said. 'For shock. I'll make it.'

The kitchen was smelly and grubby but not damaged. We sat either side of the table, Mum somehow small and low down in her chair.

'I shouldn't blame Marge,' she said, contrite. 'I'm at fault, and she's been so kind. It's been quite a day.'

'Tree-hunting?'

She hooked a straying hair behind her ear. 'Yes. Marge told me something she'd spotted in the parish records. Her uncle's churchwarden at St Biddulph's out at Matham. She drove me over. Rather a long way but worth every mile.' The hair escaped but she didn't notice. 'There it was – Maria-Ann Selworth married Joseph Kelly, 17 August 1864, and Alice was born in the October. Think of that – a shotgun wedding! Imagine the tittle-tattle . . .'

I cut in to stem the rising tide of enthusiasm: 'Why didn't you make a shopping list?'

It took a moment for her to refocus. 'I did. I lost it.'

Over the rim of my mug I saw her eyes watching me over hers. The landscape of her face was the same, but for the very first time she ceased being the capable, infuriating, interfering, steadfast Mum, always there like a rock that kept tripping me up. I saw her afresh. Someone quite separate from myself. A woman with a private life.

The sense of liberation made me almost high. 'There's something I want to ask you.'

'What's that?' She took another sip of tea.

'Why don't I call you by your first name?'

Little ripples of shock crossed her forehead. She said: 'What . . . *Augusta?*' as if I'd suggested some-

69

thing indecent. 'I've never been able to *stand* my name – pretentious rubbish!'

I nearly laughed. 'You never said.'

She shrugged.

'I could call you Gus,' I offered. 'That's nice.'

She tried it out, hissing the esses – 'Gusss' – still suspicious. 'Why?'

'You'd seem more like a friend.'

Her eyes widened. For a moment it was as if the two of us were balanced on the head of a pin. An attack of the conventions, or a sudden puff of rebellion could have blown us either way. My insides fizzed.

She said: 'Oh!' then, primly: 'And what am I to call you?'

'Why, Kelly of course! It's my name. You *gave* it to me! Stylish, remember?'

A shy grin crept across her face, struggled, and blossomed into a full-blown laugh. I had to join in. I couldn't help it. When David strolled in we were hugging our aching ribs.

He looked at us in utter surprise. 'Isn't tea ready yet? I'm *starving*!'

See the Pretty Star

GWEN GRANT

The rumour drifted through the factor like frost, chilling everyone it touched.

'Rationalisation.' That was the only word Maya remembered afterwards.

'What does it mean?' she asked Big Belle.

'It means they're going to sack people, that's what it means.'

Maya felt as if she had been hit with a piece of the wood that surrounded her machine. Her job meant everything to her. She knew it wasn't a fancy job. Drilling holes in wood all day had to be dull, but it paid. She got a wage and with that money she had started to buy new clothes.

At seventeen, it was the first time she had worked.

She was even saving for a holiday. Two weeks in Spain. It was the first time, too, that she had been able to think about a holiday.

The very thought of Spain made her want to dance. If she was rationalised, all that would go and she would be back where she'd started. Broke. No new clothes. No holiday. No Spain with Nita and Jenny and Susan.

'How are they going to choose the ones they sack?' she pursued.

Big Belle grimaced. 'Why don't you go and look

71

at the notice they've put up, instead of asking me everything? I've told you about that before.'

Maya turned away. She had only been in the factory a week when she had asked Big Belle why she had to drill holes which were then filled with wooden pegs.

'You're not here to ask questions,' Belle had snapped. 'You're here to work.'

'I only wanted . . .'

'I don't care what you wanted. You're wasting time, you are. I know you kids. Anything rather than work.'

'It's not like that at all,' she had protested, but Belle was the supervisor and Maya had seen that the big woman was taking a dislike to her.

Later, at home, she had told her mother.

'I only asked her,' she said. 'And she was really rotten about it.'

'You should have asked me. I'd have told you. Keep away from Belle. She's known for her moods.' She paused, then went on, 'Try and keep this job, Maya. We need the money.'

Maya had flounced upstairs to her room. Why did they all speak to her as if she was stupid? She knew they needed the money. She needed the money herself, never mind anyone else. And all she'd wanted to know ... she snapped her thoughts off.

Concentrate on Spain. She looked at the poster beside her bed. The hot red and orange colours enchanted her. She could almost taste them. Delighted, she had rolled on to her stomach, hugging the pillow. Spain! Oh, Spain!

Hot dark nights. Young men, yes, like the ones

on the poster. Dark eyes, thin, good-looking faces.
Grinning, she sat up. Her mother didn't need to tell
her they needed the money. She needed it, for the
experience of a lifetime!

Now, in the noisy factory, Maya could see Spain
disappearing without trace.

She waited until Big Belle had moved out of
sight, then darted from behind her machine and
waved to Susan. She could just see her friend
through the banks of machinery. After a moment
or two, Susan stepped out and waved back.

Maya pointed to the lavatories. She wanted to
talk but Susan shook her head. Big Belle was clearly
in one of her moods. When she was that way, she
patrolled the lavatories like some sort of police
sergeant.

'You've had two minutes,' she would say. 'Go on,
get off back to work.'

Belle seemed to have the ability to watch the
machines, watch the output, watch the women and
watch the lavatories all without blinking.

When tea-break came, Maya waited for her
friend.

'Have you heard?' she said.

Susan nodded.

'They've put up a notice in the main hall. Come
on, let's go and see what it says.'

When they reached the hall, it was as if everyone
had had the same idea. There was no chance
of getting close to the small piece of paper
neatly pinned in the exact centre of the green baize
board.

Big Belle came into the hall and immediately

forced her way through the crowds of women.

'Get back, get back,' she shouted. 'I'll read it to you and then you'll all know what it says.'

Her voice soared over their heads but, at the end, Maya was no wiser than before.

'Who are they getting rid of?' she asked and Susan looked at her in surprise.

'Don't you know?' Maya shook her head. Anxiety made her sharp. 'I wouldn't be asking if I knew.'

'It's last in, first out, Maya. Always has been.'

Maya felt very cold. She stood in the hall and stared at the marble tiles and huge sunburst clock and thought she was going to be sick.

'But . . . but,' she started, then stopped. There was no point. It was only fair, wasn't it, that it should be last in, first out.

But that night at home it became clear there would be others rationalised, not only the last in.

'I could lose my job as easy as winking,' her mother said.

'But you've worked there twenty-seven years.' Maya was appalled. 'They won't lay you off.'

'I'll tell you what they'll do. They'll pick and choose in each department, so keep your head down, Maya. That way you might save your job.'

'I thought it was last in, first out.'

'That's old-fashioned stuff. They'll keep the ones they want to keep and get shot of the rest and that's all there is to it. They're not bothered how long you've been there. That kind of thing's gone. Loyalty. There's no loyalty any more. It's all production now.' Her mother switched off the gas fire. 'Remember what I've said, Maya. Keep your head down and you'll be OK.'

It was at lunchtime the next day that Belle went up to her.

'Here, smart ass,' Belle started. 'You're the one always asking questions. Now, I've got one to ask you. Do you want to be on the strike committee?'

Maya put down her cup of tea.

'Do I want to be what?'

'You heard.' Big Belle turned away and bawled down the canteen, 'She's suddenly gone deaf.'

'Smart ass yourself,' Maya said with quick anger. 'I only asked what you said.'

'I'll tell you then.' Belle sat down, leaning towards the girl.

Maya watched as the big woman settled into the chair.

'Seen enough?'

'Yeah. Yeah, I've seen enough.'

'Do you want to join the strike committee?'

Maya could hear her mother's voice. 'Keep your head down and you'll be all right.'

'I thought it was all cut and dried,' she said. 'The company haven't got the money to pay so they can't pay.'

'I haven't come to answer more of your questions.' Belle snapped.

'Then sod off.' Maya was indignant. 'You can't even be civil, you can't. I'm not joining no strike committee, not unless I know what it's for and what's going to come from it.'

Belle smiled suddenly. Maya was taken aback. She realised she'd never seen the woman smile before. It made her look younger.

'OK. Look, there's no guarantees, Maya. We can try and fight for our jobs and that's all we can do.

You know what it's like these days. Everybody's beat before they start. We're all scared.' She sniffed. 'That's what's wrong, you know. We're all scared. We think if we keep quiet we'll hang on to our jobs.'

'And won't we?'

The big woman shrugged.

'Who's to say?' She stood up. 'Don't give me an answer now. Let me know tonight before you go home.'

Susan was dead against it.

'You'll be out before your toes can touch the floor, joining that lot,' she said.

'I shall be out, anyway, according to you.' Maya was curt.

She felt sad about Spain. She could see her holiday disappearing and all that fun with the girls disappearing with it. It had been a nice dream. 'Yeah,' Maya thought bitterly. 'But not for me.'

Miserably, she went back to her machine and picked up the first piece of wood. Up, over, in, drill, pull out, up, over and down.

Again and again, over and over, but at the end of it all there were bank notes in a packet. The bank notes were important. You can't live on thin air, try as you might. Up, over, in, drill, pull out, up, over and down.

At tea-break, on her way to the canteen, her mother stopped her.

'I've heard they've asked you to go on that strike committee they're getting up.'

'Yes.'

'Did you tell them where to go?'

Maya shook her head without answering.

'Why not? Was I talking to myself last night, then?'

'Mum. I haven't decided what to do yet.'

'You haven't decided.' Her mother's voice was scornful. 'You haven't decided. You remember, madam, what you'll be giving up before you start going on any strike committee. I've told you. Keep your head down and you'll keep your job.'

'You can guarantee that, can you?'

'What?'

The girl was struck by the pale sharpness of her mother's face. She could see the lines of worry scoring deep tracks over the fine skin. Her mother took off her glasses, rubbing at her eyes. She looked tired and vulnerable and Maya had an unexpected urge to put her arm around her shoulders. She wanted to tell her to go home, not to worry, to make a cup of tea and put her feet up.

'I said "What?"'

'It doesn't matter.' The girl sighed. 'It's all right, Mum.'

'You're not going to join them, then?' Her mother's face lit up.

Maya was silent a moment and then she said, 'Do you remember when I was a little girl and I couldn't sleep?'

Her mother's face softened.

'Yes.'

'When you used to open the curtains and we'd look out of the window together?'

'Yes, I remember.' The voice was wary. 'Why?'

Maya breathed deeply. The hot air in the factory smelt of oil and sawdust. It tasted of oil and resin. She looked back down the big workshop with its long aisles of machinery and its piles and piles of wood.

She looked at the solid golden mounds of sawdust beside some of the machines and at the thin, drifting, yellow mimosas of wood dust beside others.

It was all shadowed and dark, with only a few lights left on. When the break ended it would spring into brilliant life again as each machine was restarted and each woman positioned herself for work.

Then, the dark patches of oil on the floor would gleam their different colours.

'Fairy washing,' Maya murmured. When she was a child that's what she had called the quicksilver colours hidden in oil.

When the machines came on, she knew you wouldn't be able to hear yourself think. The high scream of the drills, the pudpudpud of the hammers, the shirring of the lathes and the beating, pulsing drum of the big engines would almost make the air quiver.

She picked up from where she had finished.

'We used to look through the window and you would point to that big, bright star.' She turned her face to her mother. 'You remember?'

'I've said I remember.' The words were hard and inflexible. Maya ploughed on. '"See the pretty star," you would say. "That's what to aim for, Maya. The stars".'

'It was just something to say. Something to quieten you with. It didn't mean anything.'

The girl smiled. 'I know. But it came to mean something.'

'Don't come to me when they sack you,' her mother warned, impatient, lifting a finger to point at her, to prod the air. 'Don't come crying on my shoulder. See the pretty star! You want your head looking at, Maya. That was when you were a girl. You're not a girl any longer. You're a working woman. No. No.' She waved aside Maya's words. 'Doesn't make a jot of difference if you're seventeen or seventy. When you're working, you're a woman.' She nodded, agreeing with herself. 'My word, you are.' Again, a nod. 'I would never have believed it of you. It's not as if you could pick up a job when you want it, is it? Not around here, anyway. Not with all this unemployment. What's the matter with you, don't you like work?'

Maya's lips pleated together.

'Mum,' she started. 'This job means a lot to me. It means that much, I'm prepared to fight for it. I want this job. I need it. I want to keep it. I don't want to sit there and get shoved out knowing I've done nothing to try and keep it.'

'And you'll still have done nothing to keep it when you're on that stupid committee. You'll have done plenty to lose it, though. Anyway,' her mother wound up, 'don't come looking to me for support, because you'll get none.'

'I shan't look to you for anything, don't worry.'

'And you watch who you're speaking to, Miss. You might be big on your strike committee but you still live at home.'

Maya walked away. 'Heck,' she thought. 'One minute I'm a woman, the next I'm a kid that's not allowed to say what I feel.' She kicked a pile of sawdust.

'Oy!' An indignant voice stopped her. 'What do you think you're doing? Do you think I sweep that up for fun?' The woman handed her a brush. 'You put that back, Maya, just as you found it.'

Maya swept the little pile together again. She felt like stamping on it.

The first meeting of the strike committee was in the canteen after work but it ran into immediate problems, for management switched off the lights and heat.

'This is going to be a long fight,' a voice out of the darkness said.

There were murmurs of agreement. Three of the committee were delegated to speak to management. Maya, Big Belle and a young man Maya had never seen before.

'Where do you work?' she asked him. 'I've not seen you around.'

'I'm outside. In the loading bay.'

'That's Peter,' Belle broke in. 'Everybody knows Peter.'

Maya wondered why.

As if she had said the words aloud, Peter went on, 'I was on the last strike committee. Fat lot of good that did either.'

Then they were in the director's office. Peter spoke fluently and Maya was astonished to hear herself supporting him with equal passion.

'You did well.' Big Belle was pleased with her.

Maya felt Belle had almost undermined their success. For the first time management were listening. No thanks to Belle, she thought. The big woman had an unfocused aggression and fear that had sprayed around the office like

80

pellets from a shot gun.

'You should leave the talking to us, Belle,' she began.

Belle turned on her, her mouth open in surprise.

'Why, you little . . .' She stopped. 'Now, you listen here. Just because he's wearing trousers don't mean he's better than me.' She ignored Maya's protest. 'We work in different ways. I thought you'd have known that. I thought you had more about you. All them questions you ask. All that looking for answers, wanting to know this, that and the other. I thought you might have learnt a few things, like thinking before opening your mouth.' She grunted. 'Well, you will learn, Maya, because life will teach you, and the sooner the better, if you ask me.'

'Oh yeah, life,' Maya thought. That was all they ever offered.

As the workers streamed into the canteen, ready for the big meeting, Maya searched the sea of faces for her mother. She wasn't there. She felt flat and disappointed.

Belle nudged her.

'Miss Know-it-all,' she said. 'Seeing as how you think you're so good, you can speak first.'

Maya wanted to sink into the floor and pull it over her head. She forced herself to step forward. Everything depended on this meeting. She thought of Spain. She thought of the new clothes. But, most of all, she thought of . . . 'Get on with it,' Belle's voice broke in. 'They're waiting.'

Maya started. 'When we are young,' she whispered.

'Speak up! We can't hear you!'

81

She could hear them. Their voices were so loud.

She swallowed nervously and then her mother's pale face poked round the door.

Maya grinned. She started again with new courage.

'When we are young, we reach for the stars. But when we are older, we don't ask for the stars. We only ask for our jobs.'

Her mother sat down. Slowly, she started to clap.

A Werewolf in May

ANNIE DALTON

It's a Sunday morning in May. I've had a soak in the Kaiser's bath, lazed over ritual croissants with Rosie and I'm just getting stuck into *Great Expectations* so I can finally write my essay on Estella, when the doorbell jangles.

The young policeman stammers, his voice husky with sympathetic tears and I know before he finishes his sentence.

Our flat is full of unexpected steps so all I can see is Rosie's top half: the glossy wing of her hair against the ivory of her sweater. She's clutching the potato peeler.

'I understand,' she's saying, cool, composed. 'Gerald's been trying to get through? The phone must be out of order. How kind of you to . . . We were half expecting it, you see. What dreadful things you have to . . . We mustn't keep you. Thank you so much.'

Recognising the tiny tremor in her voice for what it is, I duck into the sitting room and squash myself savagely into a corner of the white sofa, therefore leaving less space for the explosion that's coming. Then I stuff a tissue in my mouth, desperately choking back the crazy shrieks that threaten to issue through my locked jaws.

As Rosie closes the door on the tearful policeman, I erupt at last, beating the cushions like a gibbon. I'm laughing so hard I'm nearly sick. Rosie stumbles in, her eyes streaming, making similar barnyard noises.

Neither of us can speak at first but finally Rosie says, 'I need a drink. Did we leave much after the flu?'

'Not much,' I say with a significance which escapes her.

I follow her into the kitchen with its green ferns, huge church-like windows. My mother pours her booze with an unsteady hand.

'That *poor* man. The more distraught he looked, the more incapable I felt of one single natural emotion. I *am* unnatural. A cold unnatural woman.'

We sit at the white painted table in a dazzle of sunlight that's almost too bright. It's impossible to live here and not be aware of the ocean on our doorstep. I'm forever catching glimpses of it out of the corner of my eye. At night the fretting of the waves is the last sound I hear.

Our flat was once part of a posh hotel. It's spacious, rambling, every room painted by Rosie in flawless white. Lately this reminds me too much of wedding cake but I can't imagine living anywhere else. The only place I know as well is my grandparents' gruesome bungalow, and I get the shudders just remembering that. It's why Rosie, their daughter, has her addiction to white paint, white furnishings.

'He couldn't know,' I say. 'Your policeman. He was imagining a story-book granny. Lace and lavender. He didn't *know* her.'

I'm remembering Nan: the dark circles around

84

her eyes, the stifling room she hadn't left for years. Granddad measuring out her medicine; his bony hands with their ropes of veins. So kind, so patient. Only he never looked at her, never used her name. 'Here you are, Mum,' he'd say cheerily, avoiding her eyes. 'Down the hatch.'

Nan feverishly tipping the trashy jewellery into my hands when he'd gone.

'Take it, Emilia. You might never see me again. You're much prettier than Rosemary ever was.' Her eyes sly, hungry – for what? Nan's mind is a health-hazard, a twilight zone I prefer to keep out of. I just want to keep Rosie safe. I want Rosie not to listen to those poisonous outpourings, not to care.

Rosie says, 'I feel funny. Perhaps it's the whisky.'

She's the same colour as her sweater, her features sharp with anxiety. I realise Rosie's sick with shock at the death of this woman who never wanted her, who hurt her so badly, who refused to meet me until I was three.

'You're supposed to have tea for shock,' I say. 'I suppose it still *is* a shock. Even good news is a shock, you know.'

'Em, unnatural daughter though I may be, even I wouldn't go so far as to call my mother's death "good news".' Rosie has her head down, taking shuddering breaths. 'The worst thing of all,' she says, her voice muffled by her knees, 'is knowing I can *never* make it come right now.'

We wait for the kettle, listening to the steady thudding of waves at the end of the street. My heart thumps erratically as though I've drunk too much coffee.

'Even winning a Premium Bond,' I continue

irrelevantly. 'And getting married. That's a shock. They told us in Biology.'

'That I *can* believe.' Her colour is better now, her tone almost crisply normal.

Rosie doesn't believe in marriage. Or in people much. When she's not teaching at the poly, she writes books on gender. When I compare her to mothers with friends to visit and scandals to concoct over the phone, I realise how solitary, how self-contained she is.

Rosie doesn't seem to need anything except her work and our life in this flat. She says she doesn't need a man cluttering up her life. He'd slow her down, she says.

But she did, for some inexplicable reason, want a daughter, so here I am, taraa! And, as Rosie prompts me anxiously from time to time, I'm 'amazingly normal considering'.

The trouble is I don't feel normal and haven't done since the day I discovered how my highly efficient, super-cool mother came to have me.

But I can't talk to her about that.

We sit clutching scalding white cups, taking tiny medicinal sips, and Rosie says, 'Will you mind stopping on your own, Em? I'll have to go to the funeral. There's no need for you to come. It's so near your exams.'

She doesn't look at me but I feel the tidal surge through my insides all the same. I give in as I usually do. I've never been to a funeral after all. Anyway, I don't want to stay in the flat by myself.

'The exams aren't that near,' I say, cunningly. 'And I can read anywhere.'

She peers narrowly at me through her contacts. I

meet her piercing gaze with the frank sincerity I've perfected over years.

'Honestly,' I say. 'I'd like to. Otherwise I'll worry.'

This is true. It's fragile, our little ark of two. I want to keep my eye on her, in case she takes it into her head to be the one to die next.

'I'll find a phone box and call Gerald. Get it over,' says Rosie, visibly steeling herself. 'Help, Em – I haven't got anything black. Do people still wear black?'

'Will Gerald come?' I haven't seen my uncle for years. He's just a distant rumour of wealth and power; the favoured child, the son.

'If the stocks and shares can spare him.'

She puts on her classy trenchcoat, carefully ties the bronze silk scarf that reminds me of chrysanthemums and goes out, leaving me wondering why I've denied myself the comfort of going with her.

I try to read but the sentences break up under my gaze, so I go into the bathroom and run scalding water from the fat brass taps. My hands are mauve. I want to warm them.

I love our bathroom. It's big enough to dance in, if you watch your step with the potted ferns. Rosie had two basins put in, with a mirror each, so we can both brush our teeth and titivate without squabbles in the mornings. Designed *by* women *for* women, she says.

The Kaiser slept here once when it was a hotel. Rosie swears he used our bath, a regal cast-iron affair with claws. I imagine him with his helmet on, his feet sticking out the tap end while he soaped away singing something Germanic and hearty. The Kaiser wouldn't approve of Rosie.

I don't either. Not any more. Not since I guessed the truth about my father.

I dry my hands which are normally pink again and have another crack at *Great Expectations*.

Estella's mother was single too, if you haven't read the book. Miss Havisham adopted Estella for the bizarre purpose of breaking men's hearts. Miss Havisham was a jilted bride, rather past her sell-by date, with eccentric notions of decor; festoons of spiders' webs, mummified wedding feasts, that sort of thing. It's over the top Gothic stuff and completely improbable. Estella would have died in infancy from those insanitary conditions long before she got the chance to break one single heart if you ask me.

Only, after I read the book, I couldn't sleep. It was as if Estella Havisham herself was whispering breathily in my ear, warning me. *Beware*, was what I thought she said.

Beware, Emilia. Your house is as full of grim secrets as my own.

And she was right.

Because Rosie did love a man once, you see, years ago. And he took off, too, at the last minute. Rosie told me the Christmas we went down with flu. She'd staggered to the off-licence with a roaring temperature because someone told her whisky helped the symptoms, only it flushed the juicier bits of Rosie's past out instead. I don't remember much. I was rather sloshed myself. But I remember her weeping violently about green eyes and 'that charismatic bastard'.

It was a shock to realise she was capable of it, frankly. Rosie generally prefers efficiency over sentiment. There's nothing efficient about love. Love causes havoc. Look at Helen of Troy.

Anyway, this drunken confession was my first clue that there was more to Rosie than meets the eye. You'll have noticed I'm too cowardly to ask Rosie things outright. To understand why you'd have to know her; experience first-hand the prickling force field she casts around herself if I even *hint* I'd like to know who my own father was.

As if it's irrelevant. Like, 'Why would you need to know? What *good* would it do?'

So I've found myself thinking Estella has a point. That my modern mother uncomfortably resembles the Victorian Miss Havisham. Not in matters of hygiene, but in her determination to have daughters without the encumbrance of men.

And I began wondering why Rosie dresses herself in the sort of understated camouflage that would enable her to pass through an autumnal forest undetected, when from the first she dressed me in flamboyant peacock blues, fuchsia, scarlet and emerald?

It was Estella who put me on to the next important clue. 'How will you know who you are, my dear, until you know who your father is?' she murmured. 'I thought myself a beautiful princess just like you, Emilia, when all along I was a convict's daughter.'

This chilled me through and through. But it was like the story where the young bride is told, 'Never go into that locked room,' and she knows there's something sinister in there but she just has to find out what.

I waited until Rosie was at an especially long-winded meeting. But when I finally held the scrap of paper that was my birth certificate in my shaking hand, it only told me what I knew: my name and date of birth.

I felt defeated. I wondered if I had a father at all. It was tempting to believe I was the result of divine intercession, like the maidens whose luminous encounters with swans and thunderbolts Rosie would infinitely have preferred to tangling with the human male.

By the time Rosie came home I was so miserable I owned up about my snooping but she still refused to admit this 'silly father business' had any significance whatsoever.

'You needn't have been so melodramatic. You only had to ask if you wanted to see it,' she grumbled. 'And hurry, Em. Sainsburys close in an hour.'

'Just promise me,' I implored, practically clasping my hands together like a Dickens' heroine, 'that my father wasn't a murderer.'

'Not so far as *I* know,' was Rosie's crisp, terrible reply, and she grabbed her Jaeger jacket and stalked out, carrying the shopping bags.

Then it all came together in a rush.

I'd read those *Cosmo* articles about women without men who wanted children. Efficient, modern women like Rosie. I just hadn't realised their rather clinical solution applied to my own life. Until now.

Rosie really *didn't* know who my father was. Not because she'd slept with so disgracefully many men she couldn't remember, but because she'd genuinely never met him.

I don't know about you, but I'd rather be a convict's daughter any day than begin my existence in a syringe. (And before the syringe, some sort of surgical dish, I supposed, shuddering.)

If Rosie guessed my dismal thoughts as I trudged round Sainsburys after her, she refused to notice. In fact she became brighter, chattier than ever.

That night I lay in bed, blindly feeling my face with my fingertips. I could feel my body losing weight, solidity. Any minute I might dissolve like ink into the blotter of the night.

Estella appeared with her tinkling laugh, dripping candle grease. 'I warned you,' she said. 'I fear your mother intends you to break men's hearts with your beauty as Miss Havisham schooled me to do.'

'I'm not beautiful and Rosie doesn't go in for breaking hearts,' I said without conviction. 'She's a modern woman. Times change.'

But I was travelling through time myself so fast I felt sick.

I was three years old and Rosie was buttoning up my new Laura Ashley dress. 'How pretty you look. Aren't you *beautiful*, sweetheart? What a *pretty* girl.'

I was thirteen and Rosie was stepping back to admire me, her blushing self-conscious creation, insisting: 'You'll be the prettiest girl at the party, Emilia.'

I began to see why I have this problem with mirrors – well, reflective surfaces: windows, puddles, spoons. Compelled to look in every one I pass, to make sure I still physically exist. You may laugh but it genuinely surprises me to catch sight of myself laughing animatedly with my friends, looking as real as they do. It's amazing, how convincing I look . . .

The journey to Granddad's is grimmer than usual. Freezing rain that turns to sleet, then unseasonal snow. Granddad's bungalow is at the end of an unmade road. As Rosie's Beetle bounces over potholes, Granddad waits in the dark doorway, wringing his thin hands, coughing bronchially.

'Come in, Rosemary. Come in.' Before we're in the house he's rattling away about Nan's funeral as if cheerfully discussing the disposal of a stranger. It's creepy how jolly he manages to be and how fast he talks, through those rasping, wheezy struggles for air. But the look in his eyes is a scared child's. I want to hug him, shake him, tell him to shut up, tell him we love him, but he's so busy coping well he hardly sees me; has never seen me, I think.

Rosie's expression pierces me as she puts her arms tightly around his bony body to hug him hard, then says, swallowing, looking round anxiously, 'She's not still – ?'

'No, no, they took her away. To make her decent, you know. I've got a nice bit of bacon in for your lunch,' he adds, unexpectedly.

Rosie's been vegetarian for years but all she says to this *non sequitur* is, 'I'm not hungry, Dad, thanks. Is Gerald here?'

'Not till tomorrow.' Granddad's hushed tone implies that my uncle is caught up in affairs of the realm at the very least.

As I lug our cases from the car, an old man barges past with a disconcerting feral growl. His unshaven jaw only adds to my fleeting impression of some kind of geriatric werewolf.

'That's Norman from next door. Hungover as

usual,' hisses Granddad, ushering us into the stale hall. 'Maybe we should buy paper doileys to hide the cracks in the plates, before everyone gets here, what d'you think?'

That night Rosie and I share a bed for the first time since I was two. We fall asleep straight away, back to back.

Until I jerk awake with an appalling intuition.

Nan's corpse lay where I am lying now.

We are sleeping in Nan's bed; the bed she died in only hours ago. The sheets, I hope and pray, have been changed. But the bed, the bed . . .

My teeth instantly start chattering. I want to leap up screaming with the horror of it. Rosie must have been too tired to make the connection herself last night.

I try to get a grip on myself. What's the sense in two of us being awake with the creeps? And where else would we sleep?

I struggle to control my rattling jaw, breathe slowly, quelling thoughts of skulls and graves; swallowing, swallowing down the fear.

Rosie's side of the bed creaks. 'What's the matter?' she whispers.

'Nothing,' I lie. 'I'm fine.'

'I need a pee. I haven't drunk so much tea in years. But I don't want to wake Dad.'

'You won't sleep if you don't go.'

'I won't sleep anyway,' she hisses back. 'Believe me.'

That's when I *know* she knows.

'It is a bit creepy, isn't it?' I say, my body shrinking from the bedlinen as if it's imprinted with Death itself. I'm fighting a losing battle with the slippery eiderdown. We have duvets at home.

'Just a touch,' she says, with feeling.

It's so stark, so blackly comic, this situation, I experience a rush of courage, a bizarre enjoyment of the sheer awfulness of it. Rosie squeezes my hand with icy fingers.

'God, I hate that wallpaper,' she mutters. 'I can feel it staring at me in the dark. Why do we bother with families, Em? All that grotesque witter about bacon and doileys. No wonder I'm so abnormal.'

'You aren't abnormal,' I say, loyally. I suspect she is, really, but I love her just the same.

'I just wish,' I whisper daringly into the eiderdown, 'I wish I knew why you *had* me.'

There is an elongated silence. Enough, it seems, for each of us to cross the Arctic tundra and back. Slowly.

Then she says wonderingly, turning on to her back, 'You really don't know, Em?'

'How could I? You never tell me a thing.' My voice cracks with the hurt I no longer bother to hide.

'I had you,' she says slowly, 'because, when I found out I was expecting you, I wanted you more than I ever wanted anything in the world. Your father was the man. You know, the man I told you about. I thought you knew. Who did you *think* it was?'

'You mean the man who jilted you?' I exclaim, startled into a shriek. 'The charismatic bastard?'

'Sssh – *jilted*, what century do you live in, Emilia? He *walked out* on me. Don't ennoble it. And by then I was very much expecting you. So I kept you, and you turned out wonderfully, sweetie, didn't you? The best choice I made in my whole life. Are you satisfied now?'

94

'I was afraid I started life in a *dish*.'

'A dish?' I picture her smooth brow furrowing in the darkness. 'Good grief, you mean artifical – Do they do it in a dish? I imagined it was a kind of jar.'

'Well, a utensil, anyway.'

'Why ever did you think – ?'

'Because you wanted a daughter, but not love or a husband. Because you're so bloody efficient.'

More silence. The bed starts to quiver. I'm afraid it's with sobs, until I hear her witchy chuckle. When she laughs Rosie sounds remarkably like her mother. I'd forgotten those too rare times when Nan got the giggles. Was Nan laughing now, listening, applauding us on the other side of the dark? Suddenly I very much want to think so.

'The first time,' hoots Rosie, thumping the pillow. 'The very first time and bingo, you were conceived! Efficient! I didn't know what was happening till I was five months pregnant!'

This confession of female incompetence is endearing. It's also a surprising relief to know she loved the charismatic bastard, however mistakenly. I understand she doesn't care to risk such hurt again. That she needs every scrap of cool composure to hide what she imagines to be the ugly mess inside.

She hugs me hard. I smell her shampoo in the dark.

'No swan feathers then,' I say, secretly rejoicing. 'No lightning bolts after all.'

'I'm afraid not, sweetheart. But oh, his eyes, his beautiful green eyes . . .'

I wish I could see the soppy smile I know is spreading all over her face.

'But honestly, you twit, Em,' she whispers, 'if only I'd – the trouble is, sometimes I want to talk to you about – you know – things, only – you always look as if you're coping so frighteningly well.'

It's my turn to be surprised. 'Mostly I'm terrified. I must've just inherited your super-cool expression.'

'You must. It's a bloody good defence, isn't it?'

She buries her face in my shoulder, trembling, not with laughter this time.

You got it wrong, Estella, I say silently. So completely wrong. But Estella has fled away to her own candlelit realms forever, and cannot hear me.

I decide to risk telling Rosie about Miss Havisham when a cataclysmic slam announces the return of Norman the werewolf. Through plywood walls he breaks into drunken, excruciating song.

'For the night has a thousand eyes – ' he howls.

'Oh no,' whispers Rosie. 'I think I see them, snapping open all around me.'

My strangled explosions sound like a pig snorting, which sets her off.

'I mustn't,' Rosie scolds herself. 'I mustn't. What will poor Dad think? I'm a wicked woman, laughing on my mother's deathbed. I won't, I *won't* –'

For what seems like a lifetime the two of us, maybe even the three of us, frantically muffle our despicable laughter; we bury it under pillows, we smother it with our fists. We'd jam our feet down our throats if it would do any good. But nothing works. We're beyond redemption.

Unnatural women. Nan, Rosie, me.

We laugh until we hurt all over.

A Warm Safe Bed

MONICA HUGHES

We got an assignment in Holistic English today: *My Roots and What They Mean to Me*. It's to be partly a research project and partly an exercise in the 'literary convention of the essay'. The results will make up fifty per cent of our final mark, so it's pretty important.

My roots: I guess I'm lucky. My father's family is from Trinidad and my mother's is from Japan. He's a famous Caribbean musician and composer. You've probably heard of Dirk Johnson. Mum's a mathematician, the kind who doesn't deal in numbers, but mostly Greek letters that describe how the universe began and where it's going.

Parents like mine make for fascinating conversation at the breakfast table and, like I say, I'm lucky. I love every kind of music, and maths is a snap. I'm also pretty good at English, which neither of them care about at all.

Physically, my parents' genes have made me a hundred and fifty centimetres tall, and I weigh an even fifty kilogrammes in a bikini, which really becomes me. I have small bones and my skin is the colour of nicely-done toast. My eyes are dark and my hair is black and wavy, but not unmanageable. Altogether, a neat package; I'm glad I'm me.

When I explained to Mum about my assignment,

she gave me the access code to the file she calls, 'Family Album'. It's fascinating: Mum's family history, generation by generation back to Osaka, Japan. Pictures of her grandparents' wedding, with him in a stiff-collared black suit and her in a gorgeous kimono, her piled-up hair full of ornaments. Mum's mother and father were married in Clapham, and their clothes were ordinary, only a bit old-fashioned.

Dad's father ran away from Trinidad to Liverpool, so there's not a lot of history and pictures of his side of the family in the file, just a couple of snaps of him as a young man and the wedding photographs which I recognised, of course, from the holograms on the living-room wall.

The next item was their marriage certificate: June 4, 1992, and my birth certificate, November 3, 1994. Me, Naoko, the only child.

'Didn't you want a boy as well?' I used to ask, when I was younger, thinking it might be fun to have a kid brother to boss around. But Mum and Dad always shook their heads and said they were lucky to get me.

My Roots and What They Mean to Me. I could write ten pages, I guess, but I knew I wouldn't get high marks for research that way. I decided that since I had access to 'Family Album', I'd look for an interesting angle. I wasn't actually snooping. At least it didn't seem that way at the time. But when I came to Mum's personal medical history I just peeked. Honest, that's all.

Surprise! Wow! In 1991, before I was born, before Mum had even met Dad, she had had a hysterectomy. If it meant what I thought it meant then Mum couldn't have possibly had any babies. She couldn't have had *me*.

I'm adopted! That was my first thought, my head in a whirl. But my eyes, my high cheekbones, the dimple just like Mum's, all denied that possibility. If you'd overlaid a transparency of Mum and one of Dad, the resulting double image was ME.

I had just enough presence of mind to exit the program properly before resetting the privacy code and switching off. Then I went for a long walk, round and round the apartment blocks, my heart pounding like mad and my hands all sweaty, like before a history exam. I thought up some pretty wild scenarios as I walked, like Dad having an affair with Mum's twin sister, and Mum nobly adopting the baby – though, as far as I knew, Mum had no sisters at all, much less a twin. *Who am I?* I asked the dustbins and the skinny trees. *Where did I come from?*

Naturally the dustbins and trees had no answer and, in the end, totally confused, with my knees trembling partly from all that pavement pounding and partly from sheer nerves, I did what I should have done in the first place. I went into the kitchen where Mum was chopping vegetables and chicken for supper.

'Mum, where do I *really* come from?'

She laid the chopper down on the block and stared at me, her face so like mine. 'Naoko, what do you mean? You know who your grandparents are and your great . . .'

'I don't mean that. I mean me, myself.' And I explained about peeking into her medical file. At the expression on her face I felt about fifty centimetres high. She looked shocked, outraged, and maybe a little scared. What horrible secret *was* there about me?

'Sorry, Mum,' I muttered. 'I guess I shouldn't have.'

'Slice the mushrooms,' was all she said, her lips tight, putting a knife into my hand.

We worked together in a silence broken only by the whack of Mum's cleaver on the block. 'You are our very own child,' she said at last. 'My ovum. Your father's sperm. You are truly ours. But you had a surrogate mother, that's all.'

'I see,' I said, not seeing at all. I sliced the mushrooms into thin, even slices with great concentration, as if my life depended on it. I just stared at those mushrooms, so I knew each pinky-brown gill by heart. When I'd finished and Mum had begun the stir-fry, I ran to my room and looked up 'surrogate' in the dictionary.

Surrogate: a substitute, a deputy.

Surrogate mother: a woman in whose uterus the zygote (fertilized egg) of another couple is implanted and raised to maturity.

Surrogate Laws: see R. versus Hepplethwaite, 1991.

I put the book back on the shelf and thought about it. Me. 'Implanted and raised to maturity.' It was like a bad dream. I'll wake up and it'll just be a bizarre dream, I told myself. Or a joke. Mum's just having me on.

If it *were* true, there was still one major problem, so I brought it up at supper, kind of testing Mum. If it *were* a joke, she'd have to tell me then.

'How can an egg possibly get fertilized before it's put into the surrogate mother?'

Dad choked, gulped his guava juice and choked again.

'Really, Naoko!'

'Sorry, Mum, but I need to know. How does it?'

'You've heard of test-tube babies, haven't you?' Dad wiped his eyes on his napkin.

'Which is a misnomer,' Mum put in severely. 'As you well know, Dirk. Technically, Naoko, you were conceived in a Petri dish.' She didn't say any more and I knew she was still hurt that I'd snooped in her private file.

'Thanks, Mum,' I said weakly. So it was true. There was something particularly real and scientific and definite about a Petri dish. I thought about it, as I silently stacked the plates in the dishwasher. A *Petri* dish!

'Conceived in a *dish*!' I said to my reflection in the bathroom mirror as I brushed my teeth. 'There's romance for you!'

It was the kind of situation that wo ʾu make a great joke. I imagined heading my essay: *My Roots in a Dish*. Or possibly *The Dish and I*. But all the time my brain was being flip and funny, inside my stomach was trembly and full of butterflies.

I'd always known that my parents really loved each other, romantically as well as being good and favourite friends, and it had always given me a warm glow to think about *me*, toasty skin and wavy hair, music and maths, like the seal of approval on their love.

Now that was all gone. Zip. Finished. Sure, I still had two loving parents who'd raised me since I was born. But I couldn't relate to that Petri dish. No way! That was science. As sterile and impersonal as the laboratory where I supposed it happened. I jumped into bed and lay there, wondering what had happened to my secure world.

When Mum came in to kiss me good night I didn't link my hands behind her neck and pull her down on top of me in a bear hug the way I always did, even though I was almost fifteen and really too big for bear hugs. I lay on my back and looked up at her, and she looked down at me, a little sadly, the way I felt inside, as if she were my reflection.

'I suppose you had to bottle-feed me, too,' I said, accusingly.

'I certainly did not!'

'Did I have a surrogate *nurse* too?' I hadn't meant for the words to sound that odious, but they did and Mum turned away to the window, pretending to fix the curtain. She is very stoical, the way Japanese people are still brought up to be, and she *never* shows her emotions unless she wants to.

After a while fixing the curtain she said, very softly, so I could hardly hear her, '*I* nursed you, Naoko. The doctor gave me hormones and I nursed you for six months.'

'Oh,' was the only thing I could think of to say. Afterwards I thought I could have said I was sorry and that it was all right, but just then I was angry and I wanted an excuse to stay angry.

Mum turned back from the window. She kissed my forehead and I think she paused, just for a second, in case I should pull her down into a bear hug, but I wouldn't. She straightened up, said, 'Good night, Naoko,' and slipped out of the room like a quiet, drooping shadow.

I lay awake, my hands behind my head, staring at

the ceiling, thinking about my mother. My surrogate mother, I mean. The one who had nourished me, with whom I had spent the first nine months of my life. I wondered what she was like. Would she be Oriental, like Mum? Or Caribbean, like Dad? I wondered if she'd have minded dreadfully having to give me up after nine months of pregnancy and labour and all that stuff? I had been a beautiful baby. I'm not just saying that. I know it's true because of everyone's reactions to my baby pictures in the living room. If I had been she, I'd *never* have given me up. I couldn't.

I lay, staring at the ceiling, as the clock numbers turned briskly over from 23:00 to 01:05 to 02:10. Now I felt rejected. By Mum and Dad who had caused me to be created in a Petri dish. And by the person I was beginning to think of as 'my real mother'.

What sort of woman would raise another couple's baby and then give it back, newborn and gorgeously, miraculously, alive? Perhaps she was a noble friend, sacrificing her life to bring happiness to Mum and Dad. I liked that idea and I wondered if Mum would tell me if I asked her.

What was she like? Perhaps she was an artist. Or maybe a famous writer. Did I get my love of language from her? After all, I argued to myself, you can't be an intimate part of a person for nine whole months and not be influenced by them. Maybe she read poetry to me before I was born. I *love* poetry most passionately and I write some, though I don't feel like showing it to anyone, not yet.

Did she ever think of me, my surrogate mother?

Did she miss me? *Would she like to see me again?* With this momentous question, I sat up in bed. Oh, yeah. My brain worked furiously, imagining our meeting. Then I finally fell asleep.

Of course I overslept, so getting ready for school was a terrible rush. What with sleepiness and trying to plan a strategy it was hard to concentrate, even in maths.

'Is anything wrong, Naoko?' Mrs Whittaker asked after I'd missed a queston for the third time. Little did she know!

Mum wouldn't be home from the university until two hours after school was out, so I went to the public library and read up on Surrogate Law (R. versus Hepplethwaite). Complicated stuff, but useful. I ran home with a complete plan in my head.

As soon as Mum got in the house I let her have it straight. 'I want to visit my mother, Mum. I mean my surrogate mother.'

She winced. 'I know who you mean, Naoko. But I don't know where . . .'

'There's a register,' I informed her. 'Department of Health. If she's willing, the law says I can.'

'The *law*?'

'1991. The Crown versus Hepplethwaite.' My voice faded at the expression on her face, as if I'd just hit her. 'I just want to *see* her, Mum. After all, she is my . . .'

'I *do* understand, Naoko. I *think* I do. You don't have to invoke the law.' She swallowed and looked at me helplessly for a minute. I'd never seen Mum not in control before. But I hardened my heart. What I had to do was more important than other people's feelings.

'You know I'll help,' she went on. 'I'll . . . I'll phone the clinic. Her address will be on file there. It will take much less time than going through the bureaucracy.'

'Thank you, Mum.' I hugged her, but she drew back.

'She still has to say she's willing,' she warned me.

'She will be,' I said confidently, looking at my baby picture smiling at me from the wall. How could she say no? I could see our meeting now. It would be *wonderful*. She'd cry, maybe, just a little. And then we'd talk and talk . . .

Mum must have pulled all sorts of strings because, two days later, there was a message on the fax machine. Mrs Geraldine Muncy would meet me in the Oriental Tearooms at the Tottenham Shopping Mall at four o'clock the very next day.

I was so excited I couldn't eat, though I was also a bit disappointed that she had invited me to meet her on neutral territory rather than in her own house, where I could see her family photographs, the kind of books she read, her taste in decorating, all the little clues I could use to build up her identity. My *mother*.

'It's a complicated trip.' Mum frowned over the map. 'A bus and two train changes. Perhaps I could get a substitute lecturer and drive you.'

'Oh, *Mum*. I'm not a child any more. I can handle it.' I knew I was safe from an offer to escort me from Dad. He was just setting out on a gig up north. In any case, this was between us women. Me and Mum. And me and my new-found mother.

Mum still looked worried. 'I'll give you enough

105

money so you can take a taxi if it gets too difficult.'

'Don't fuss, Mum.' Though I tucked the taxi money safely away in my purse, I knew I'd never use it. This was a genuine adventure, the search for my *real* roots. I could hardly wait for next morning.

I skipped the last class of the day to make sure I had enough time to get to Tottenham for the appointment. Mum was right. It was a dreadful trip, and by the time I'd fought my way on to the third grotty, graffiti-decorated train I was beginning to wish I'd been less stubborn about taking a taxi.

I stared at the blackness beyond the dirty windows and saw my mother in my imagination's eyes. Tall. Blonde and elegant. *Very* cultured, but understanding that a person might sometimes like to decorate their room in purple and silver foil and play pop music loud enough to vibrate their ribs and send shivers down their spine. Sympathetic *and* gracious.

I imagined our meeting in exact detail, as the train rattled and swayed. It was so clear I could smell her perfume, mysterious, French, instead of the bitter, sour smell of the Underground. Her hands would feel very soft and cool in mine.

'My dear, I've waited so long for this moment . . .' And her deep, blue eyes would sparkle with tears.

I found myself smiling, my lips forming the words, 'Me too, Mother,' and looked up to catch the hard eyes of three thin-faced boys, their dirty, blond hair curled into dreadlocks, staring at me. After that I kept my hands in my pockets, my eyes on my feet and, when I was shoved, I shoved back, until at last the doors slid open at the right station.

The boys followed me off the train and into an aged lift, which rattled asthmatically up to the surface and spewed us out in to a street, dingy and covered with litter. I had a moment's panic, but fortunately the mall I was looking for was just up the road. I walked briskly towards it, leaving the dreadlocked youths jeering on the corner. It was two minutes after four. Lucky I'd thought to skip that last class.

I pushed open the door of the Oriental Tearooms and looked around. It was an old-fashioned place with upholstered banquettes along the walls, red curtains and a jungle of hanging plants. Most of the tables were already occupied by little old ladies in the kind of hats I'd only seen in historical movies.

Most of them were in twos or threes, but my eyes were immediately drawn to one woman sitting alone. She was wearing a grey suit of fine wool and her silk blouse matched the dusty rose of her earrings, which in turn went wonderfully well with the coronet of blonde hair on top of her head. She had a lean face, rather like an aristocratic greyhound, and her hands were beautifully mani-cured, her nail polish exactly matching the pink of her blouse.

The second I saw her I knew who she must be. I hid my bitten nails in my doubled-up hands and walked towards her table, my heart pounding furiously. She got up as I approached and smiled. *This is it*, I thought.

'I'm just on the way, if you're looking for a table.' She picked up a briefcase from the chair opposite and walked towards the door. Even her walk was like a fashion model's.

I stood among the chattering women and the teacups, my mouth still frozen in a stupid half-smile, the words, 'Mother, I'm Naoko, your daughter!' on my tongue. I felt like a total idiot.

Then the corner of my eye caught a movement. A woman waving. At me? Did she mean *me*? I gulped and stared. She was the largest woman I had ever seen, like the 'befores' in all the before-and-after ads of Fit Clubs rolled into one. She was wearing a tent of handwoven fabric, striped in shades of brown and orange, with beads on top. Strings of beads.

For an instant I stood frozen, wondering if it would be possible to pretend I hadn't seen the frantically waving hand; then Mum's training took over and my feet led me across the room to the table in the corner. My lips formed the question, 'Mrs Muncy?' while my brain was still contemplating escape.

'Yeah, that's right. Sit down, dearie, and let's take a look at you.' Her voice was small and breathless and seemed to come from a long way inside. She laid the book she had been reading down on the table. At least I've got one thing right, I thought. She loves literature, just like me.

I peeked curiously at the cover. The jacket illustration was of a woman in a full skirt, with off-the-shoulder ruffles, crouching by a chair, while a man in knee-breeches appeared to be trying to tear open her bodice.

'Sit, sit,' Mrs Muncy urged. 'I ordered the cream tea. Hope that's what you fancy. You look as if you could stand a bit of feeding up.'

'I've got small bones, and Mum . . .' I stopped and didn't know how to go on. I had had so many questions, and they had all fled in the reality of my 'mother'. Tea came. She poured. We slathered jam and synthetic cream on to hard yellow scones.

'So you're Naoko?'

'Yes, ma'am. Do you . . . can you remember me?'

She laughed, a deep chuckle that bubbled out of her throat. 'How old are you, love? Fourteen? Give us a break.'

I could feel myself blushing and scrabbled in my purse. 'I brought one of my baby pictures.'

She looked at it briefly and handed it back. 'There were so many. Babies all look alike, you know. No character. Not till later. That's why they have to label them at birth. Now you – I can see that you've got character now. Though you certainly *are* skinny.'

I latched on to what was important. 'So many? Do you mean I wasn't your only . . . I mean, you had . . .?' I stopped and blushed. I couldn't stop thinking about that Petri dish!

'Surrogate babies?' It obviously didn't bother her a bit. 'Bless you, I must have had eight. Or was it nine? I was just a natural mother, the doctors said.'

'Could I ask . . . if it isn't rude . . . *why*?'

'The pay, my dear. After my husband died I needed the money. He had great business dreams, did Rog, and when he was gone I was stuck with the bills. I didn't have much of an education, not enough to get a decent job. My fault really, I just found school a dead bore. I couldn't make enough waitressing to pay off Rog's debts, not in a million years. Then this offer came along, an advert on the

109

telly, it was, and I grabbed it. I was a health nut back then, though you'd never know it now, would you? No smoking or drinking, vegetarian, herb tea, all that. They said I had the healthiest babies of all the mums they ever had.'

'Didn't you mind most awfully having to give me up?'

She shook her head and popped another cream-laden scone into her mouth. Her eyes wandered round the room as she tried to put into words what she meant. She licked the cream and jam from roly-poly fingers, laden with cheap silver and turquoise rings.

'It's like . . .' She struggled for the right words. 'Like a farmer raising chickens. Nothing personal. I did a good job, no drinking or drugs. Lots of sleep. Nine months later, there was a healthy baby for a couple who otherwise wouldn't have one. After a bit of a rest I'd volunteer for another implant.'

Implant, I thought. Like a *tooth*. The vision of my imaginary mother faded into the dirty, red curtains that draped the walls. There was nothing left to say. I gulped my tea, hot and tarry, the tannin coating my teeth with fur, thinking of an excuse to leave.

'Anyway, it was real nice of you to come by and look me up. I appreciate it. You're the first who's bothered.'

Something in her voice made me realise that inside the bulk was a lonely woman, with nothing to give a meaning to her life any more. It was all in the past, the good she had done. Perhaps that was the statement she had let her body make: the shapeless-ness of her life, with nothing to look forward to but the Oriental Tearooms and bodice-ripping romances.

I swallowed. 'Would you like me to come again?' I asked nobly, dreading the thought of the three trains and the stuffy boredom of the Tearooms.

She looked at me, her head on one side like a bird's. 'I don't think that'd be a good idea, love. But thanks for the thought.'

I felt as if I'd been reprieved. I glanced at my watch. 'I'd better be going if I'm to be home in time for supper.'

She buttered and creamed the last scone. 'Thanks for coming, ducks.'

'Thank *you*.' I stood awkwardly, feeling that there ought to be more drama to this goodbye. She popped the scone in her mouth and I threaded my way between the tables to the front desk and asked the way to the nearest taxi rank. It was only as we inched our way through the after-work traffic that I realised that maybe Geraldine Muncy thought I was just thanking her for the tea, instead of for my life. But it was too late to turn back and make that clear.

It had all been the most dreadful mistake. I stared blankly out of the cab window and wished with all my heart that I could roll time back to the moment when I began my essay. If only I hadn't peeked in her personal file. If only . . .

Back home I'm struggling with my essay: *My Roots and What They Mean to Me*. Struggling too with disappointment, alienation, all sorts of big words that add up to the fact that I'm no longer the same person I was a week ago when we were handed this assignment. And I'm not a bit happy or comfortable with my new self.

111

I look back through the 'Family Album' material. At the pictures of Mum and Dad's wedding. Me in Mum's arms. On Mum's knee. Playing with her on the slides. Then I bawl my eyes out for a bit.

As I wash my face I stare in the mirror and think about my beginnings. The Petri dish and Geraldine Muncy, and my dreams of a perfect relationship that didn't exist, that could never exist, except in my imagination. That wasn't even important. You dummy, I say to my reflection, and climb into bed.

The womb is a bit like a bed, I think, after a bit. A warm safe bed. But nine months is plenty long enough to stay there. I tell myself firmly that it's time to grow up and get on with the exciting business of living my real life.

When Mum comes in to say good night I'm lying on my back with my hands behind my head. She stops by my bed and looks down at me. Her face is pinched, sorrowful.

'Are you all right, Naoko?'

'I think so, Mum.'

'I'm *so* sorry.'

'It's all right. I was dumb, that's all.'

'Nothing bothering you now?'

'Just . . .' I hesitate. 'I'll be fifteen next week, Mum. Do you think fifteen is too old for bear hugs?'

Parents' Day

JEAN URE

When I was at school there were three girls who impressed me enormously. The first was Flick Taylor, the games captain, who played cricket like a demon and once shattered someone's teeth with a full toss. (It was an all-girls' school, and I suppose she was the nearest thing to a man that I could find.) The second was Barbara Ballard, who was a year above me and wore a tooth brace which gave her a sexy sort of lisp. The third was Caroline Nightingale.

Caroline and I were in the same class. What so impressed me about her – more, far more, than Janice Jannaway's long silver hair or Pam Wardle's breasts or even Chloë Chandler's claim to fame (she was second cousin to a film star) was her quiet air of quality.

Linden Hall, being for 'daughters of the clergy', was a quality school, but that didn't mean that all of its pupils lived up to expectations. I most certainly didn't, being small, squat and spotty, gauche and giggly and academically hopeless. (I once got ten out of a hundred for Religious Instruction which, all things considered, took a bit of doing. Miss Pretty said, 'I am flabbergasted, Jacqueline! Whatever will your father think?' My father probably didn't think anything. He was too busy preaching

113

the word of God to be bothered by such minor matters as his daughter's education. It wasn't, after all, as if I were a son.)

Caroline was the exact opposite of me in almost every way. She was tall and graceful, with clear, pale skin, never a spot in sight, and far too dignified to be a giggler. Academically she was good enough to have won a scholarship, though this was something I only discovered years later. None of us was aware of it at the time. You had to be poor as well as clever to win scholarships to Linden Hall, and the school didn't believe in branding people as either. All we knew then was that when it came to exams you could depend on Caroline being up there amongst the top three. Not actually top; I don't ever remember her coming top, but then it wasn't her style ostentatiously to excel. She seemed content to remain in the background – to be what Miss Kitchins, our head-mistress, called, 'a good, steady, all-rounder'.

Caroline wasn't exactly what you could have called popular – you needed to be a bit more pushy to gain popularity amongst our mob – but she was universally held in respect. Every year without fail we used to vote her vice-captain of the form to Chloë's captain. I daresay we felt that Chloë, being so flighty (connected to the world of entertainment), needed a bit of ballast to keep her steady; and Caroline was generally held to be the sanest and most sensible of us.

I thought, in those days, that I was alone in the fascination I felt for her – I mean, in my case it was obvious. I was so scatty, so dim, so generally dismal. 'Bit of a flibbertigibbet, I'm afraid, Jacqueline.' It was only natural that I should look at cool, calm, competent Caroline with longing. Not envy; I never felt that. I just enjoyed the sheer sensual pleasure of contemplating her in much the same way, I imagine, as people enjoy contemplating the Queen. I never realised till some years after leaving school that others beside myself had been intrigued by her. Even Pam, she of the wonderful big knockers (34C at the age of fourteen!) confessed to me that, 'I used to like to sit and watch her, in assembly . . . she was always so wonderfully *above* it all. She made the rest of us seem such dross.'

I have just pulled out my old school magazines and looked through them to see how often Caroline's name appears. Quite a few times, as it happens; more than I had thought. Mine appears once: 'Jacqueline Vigurs was reserve.' Caroline, on the other hand, is mentioned as playing for almost all of the games teams: under-13s netball, under-14s netball, junior netball, senior netball, under-15s hockey, 1st XI hockey . . . the list goes on. I hadn't realised just how much of an all-rounder she was. But that was typically Caroline: *shine quietly* could almost have been her motto.

The one field where she didn't shine was drama; there is absolutely no mention of her in any single one of the school productions: *The Snow Queen, The Importance, Romeo and Juliet, Through the Looking Glass*. She is, however, mentioned as winning the Helen Frazer Memorial Trophy (for essay writing) and gaining an open scholarship to Girton College, Cambridge (the only one of our year to go there, in spite of not being ostentatiously brilliant). She also produced an article for the French Club – *in French*

115

– and one for the Science Club with the title, *Picking Mushrooms on the Playing Field*.

And then there is the poem she wrote.

The poem is called, 'My Mother', and from first to last – but in the most restrained of language, nothing in the least bit mawkish – it is a song of praise. It ends,

> 'My mother is everything to me,
> Everything I am, I owe to her.
> She is, quite simply,
> My Mother.

At the foot it says, 'by Caroline Nightingale, Snr IIA'.

I remember that poem. I remember we all had to write one for a project on Home Life set by Miss Easton, our English mistress. (My daughter doesn't refer to members of staff as mistresses; to her they are teachers. Every time I say mistress she giggles or groans, depending on mood, and says, 'Mum, really!' She associates the word mistress with things sexual. Also, she calls me Mum. She can't believe I called my mother Mummy for seventeen years. It seems to her quite incredibly childish. We thought it rather common, in my day, to say Mum.)

Miss Easton picked out Caroline's poem as being not only the best-written but also as portraying 'an exceptionally close relationship between mother and daughter'. She seemed to think the rest of us exhibited a somewhat cavalier, take-it-or-leave-it attitude, which at that time we probably did. We were fourteen, overprivileged (most of us), away from home, what did we want with mothers?

Caroline's poem put us to shame. Also, it rather

embarrassed us; we didn't know how to cope with such overt devotion. Mothers were all right, and of course one wouldn't want to be without them but, as Pam rather tartly said, 'They are not *paragons*.' (Pam at that time was waging bitter war with her own mother, I recall, on the subject of strapless evening gowns, which Mrs Wardle quite unreasonably, in Pam's view, and in ours – we took enormous pride in Pam's knockers – held to be unsuitable wear for a fourteen-year-old.)

'And anyway,' – Janice Jannaway, I think it was who said it – 'if her mother is so flaming marvellous, why don't we ever see her?'

All *our* mothers, and sometimes fathers, too, though not in my case, turned up with dreary regularity at Open Day, Speech Day, Sports Day, Parents' Day; there simply wasn't any keeping them away. We knew that Caroline's father couldn't be there because she hadn't got a father, he had died before she had come to Linden Hall, but you certainly would have thought her mother would have showed.

I asked Caroline once, just casually, how it was that she managed to keep her away – implying, so that it shouldn't sound like criticism, how terribly lucky she was – and she said that the reason her mother didn't come was that, 'She's not awfully good at travelling.' I thought she meant that she got car sick, as I always did on long journeys (it used to make my father furious) but Chloë said she had heard that Mrs Nightingale was some kind of invalid and lived in a wheelchair.

We all said, 'How perfectly frightful,' and felt that it went some way to excusing the poem, because after all if you had a mother in a wheel-chair you would feel almost duty bound to be devoted to her. I pictured Caroline's mother as being terribly wan and elegant, terribly refined in spite of her disabilities (whatever they might be: Chloë didn't offer any details). I thought she would probably be rather frail and fragile, in a faded-beauty way, like the Lady of the Camellias. I thought of my own mother, all hale and hearty and pink and plump, forever rushing round the parish in a hectic flush or buried upside down in a flowerbed in a sea of mud, and I couldn't help thinking how much more romantic it would be if *she* were frail and fragile and in a wheelchair. Caroline's invalid mother began to fascinate almost as much as Caroline herself.

And then there came that Parents' Day which I suppose we shall all of us always remember. On Parents' Day people's parents arrived in droves. They gossiped and mingled, and fraternised with the staff, before finally 'taking tea' (Miss Kitchins always referred to it as 'taking tea') in Big Hall. We were sixth formers that year and expected to act as stewards, generally being helpful and pointing people in the right direction; and then, during tea, to stand behind the trestle tables manning the tea urns or circulating with plates of cakes and sand-wiches.

I was put, with Caroline, behind a tea urn at the far end of the hall, with Janice and Pam nearby, handing out plates and napkins and offering uninformed guesses as to what things might be. (It was frequently far from obvious: Linden Hall might have been quality, but its food would have disgraced one of Her Majesty's prisons. Of course, it may be different these days.)

Business at our end of the hall was not particularly brisk; we were more in the nature of reserve supplies than mainstream fodder. During the intervals of activity we stood, bunched together, idly commenting on the people present – which is to say, Pam, Janice and I commented, Caroline, as always, exercised restraint. Miss Kitchins would have had a fit if she could have heard the rest of us.

'Who on earth is that frightful tart in the fake furs?'

'My dear! Will you *look* at the creature in black!'

Of course we all groaned in pretended agony at the sight of our own parents, or my mother, in my case.

'Look at her! Done up like a Christmas pudding!'

'Never mind yours!' wailed Pam. 'What about mine? Did you ever see anything like it?'

I remember that I was about to remark that I couldn't see anything wrong with Pam's mother (any more, I daresay, than she could with mine) when Janice sidled up and out of the side of her mouth hissed, 'Don't look now, but I think that woman over there is pissed.'

Naturally, we looked immediately. I don't quite know what I expected, never having seen anyone who was drunk except on television, where they tended to roar and hiccup and fall over. All I thought was, what a gas . . . on Parents' Day! And a *mother*, to boot! A father one might have understood, especially if it were one of the few non-clergy. Fathers were renowned for their lunch-time quaffing. But a *mother* . . .

'Where?' whispered Pam. 'Which one?'

'That woman in the blue coat.'

At first sight there didn't seem anything out of the way about the woman in the blue coat. She was a bit dumpy and frumpy – permed hair which had obviously been done specially for the occasion, because it hadn't yet reached the stage of what my mother called 'dropping'; high-heeled shoes which had probably also been bought specially, judging by the shiny newness of them; lumpy black handbag dangling from her arm; not someone you would have looked twice at.

It was only after you *had* looked twice that you began to see what Janice meant. She wasn't roaring or hiccuping, but she kept wobbling on her high heels. She was talking – or trying to talk – to an immensely tall, thin man in a dog collar who towered over her by several inches so that she had to crane her head to look at him. It would have been better if she'd been able to take a step backwards, but after making two or three attempts and almost coming to grief she gave it up as being, presumably, too dangerous.

I remember Pam and I started to giggle – it was like a scene from a comedy show, this little dumpy woman tottering on her high heels. It would have helped if the dog collar had moved backwards, but of course it was all right for him being so much taller. *He* only had to bend forward.

We stood watching as the dumpy woman risked another try and went cannoning into a mother standing directly behind her. Both the dumpy woman and the mother half turned to apologise. As they did so, the dumpy woman's handbag went flying out and walloped another mother, standing at her elbow. The dumpy woman spun round, tea cup in hand, lost her balance, fell against the dog collar and liberally drenched him in a cascade of hot tea. Pam and I were giggling fit to bust.

'Honestly!' said Janice. 'She must be tanked to the eyeballs!'

And then it was that the really awful thing happened. From where we were we could see it quite plainly: the dumpy woman started to cry. Not in a loud, drunken fashion, just very quietly and helplessly as if everything had become too much for her. And suddenly it wasn't funny any more, it was ghastly and pathetic and really most dreadfully embarrassing – well, I found it embarrassing, and I suspect the others did, too. I remember Pam stopping laughing as abruptly as I did, and Janice just standing, with her mouth gaping open. Everyone was just standing. A great hush had come over the hall; as if even in the furthest-flung corners they were aware that something was wrong. And then – and this is the bit which is indelibly engraven on my memory; the rest might fade, but never this – Caroline, who so far hadn't said a word, stepped out from behind the tea urn, made her way across the hall, put an arm round the woman's shoulders and quite clearly, not minding who heard her, said, 'Come on, Mum!'

As Janice said afterwards, 'You could have knocked me down with the proverbial.'

Of course we discussed it; how could we not?

'So *that's* her wonderful mother –'

'She's not an invalid at all!'

'Well, she's not in a wheelchair –'

'She's certainly not *normal*.'

'Do you suppose – ' this, in awed tones, from Pam – 'do you suppose she's an actual P/A?'

Long silence. Then, bleatingly, from me (always so slow to catch on), 'What's a P/A?'

'An alkie,' said Janice, 'in a word.'

Later – Caroline wasn't there, she had presumably accompanied her mother back home – Miss Kitchins came to speak to us. She said that no doubt we had noticed that Caroline's mother had been taken unwell, and she did most sincerely hope, when Caroline returned, that she could trust us to be kind and understanding and above all *discreet*. We understood what she meant: she didn't want us to refer to it. We probably wouldn't have done, anyway; we wouldn't have known how. But in any case it was generally agreed that Caroline had risen most nobly to the occasion (even if she had addressed her mother as Mum).

'After all,' as Chloë pointed out, 'she didn't *have* to act the way she did. She could just have hung back and waited for someone else to take action, then we wouldn't ever have known.'

'If that had been my mother,' said Janice, 'I'd have died.'

We couldn't help wondering whether Caroline would be brave enough to come back. We were none of us sure that we would, in her place, but Caroline turned out less of a coward, in every way, than the rest of us. She came back, one week later, and we all bent over backwards to be as normal as possible and simply pretend the incident had never occurred. I thought we managed rather well; at any rate Caroline herself seemed no different from how she had been before, unless perhaps a bit more reserved. But it was hard to say; she was never what you would call outgoing.

A year later I left school and went to secretarial college; a year after that, Caroline went up to Cambridge. I never saw her again. I always used to go back for the annual reunions – I don't go so often now, I haven't the time, or perhaps the inclination – and I always looked for her, but she was never there. The last reunion I went to was five years ago. It was a special one, because it was the centenary of the Old Girls' Association. ('Eugh! Sick!' said my daughter when she heard where I was going.) Everyone from our year was there – except Caroline. We were all talking about her, wondering where she was and what she was up to. (It was then that Pam, tits more massive than ever, confessed about sitting and watching her in morning assembly.) Needless to say, someone brought up the incident with her mother.

'Do you remember?' How could we not? 'So *hideous* for her!'

'You'd really have to love someone,' said Pam. 'I'm not sure that my beastly brat would stand up for me like that.'

None of us was sure our beastly brats would stand up for us as Caroline had stood up for her poor drunken mother.

I'd missed the last few reunions and was almost beginning to forget about Caroline and the fascination she had once held for me. Then, just a couple of weeks ago, I was doing some ironing and switched on the radio for something to listen to, and there was this man interviewing some actress who'd just come back from a tour of something or other but more importantly had written a book which had just won a major prize – the Whitbread, I think it was. I'm not very well up in the world of literature. But anyway, whatever it was it was the book they were mainly talking about. It was called *Mother's Child* and was largely – or so suggested the interviewer – autobiographical.

'The heroine's father, a clergyman, dies when the heroine is six years old. Her mother commits suicide while the heroine is at university. Both these things, I believe, happened to you?'

The actress agreed that they had.

'You dedicate the book, "To my mother, who made all things possible." The heroine also uses these words, right at the end of the book. May one take it that you and the heroine are one and the same?'

Not entirely, said the actress, but there were certain common elements.

'Your mother was of great importance to you?'

'I owe her everything.'

Just like Caroline, I thought. And it was only then that the penny dropped . . . *Caroline*! Could it be? (But Caroline *acting*? It was the last thing I should have thought of in connection with her.)

'. . . devastated,' she was saying, 'when my mother took her own life, but yet at the same time strangely . . . liberated, almost. It seems a terrible thing to say, but it was as if, suddenly, for the first time, I was free to be *me*.'

'And yet you loved your mother dearly? I quote from chapter ten, the poem written by the heroine, "My Mother" –'

Of course, I knew the poem. She had used it, word for word.

'The heroine writes that when she is fourteen. Two years later occurs the incident which is perhaps central to the book, where the heroine's mother makes a really quite heartbreaking effort to overcome her fear of leaving home – agoraphobia, I suppose one would call it – in order to attend an event at her daughter's school, Willow Grove. Reflect that this is a woman who's suffered several breakdowns since the death of her husband, she's totally unused to mixing in company or travelling more than fifty metres from her own house but, on this occasion, for her daughter's sake she's determined to behave, as she says in a letter to her daughter, "Like a real mother, for once." Unfortunately, she makes the fatal mistake of trying to give herself Dutch courage out of a bottle, and the result is disastrous . . . "My mother, reeling and hiccuping in the midst of all my schoolmates' posh parents."'

Oh, Caroline! She didn't reel and hiccup – and we weren't *that* posh.

'In the book,' went on the interviewer, 'the heroine wrestles with her conscience, whether to disown her mother or go to her rescue. She finally goes to her rescue, but she says, "In that moment, I hated my mother."'

Hated? But she had said it with such gentleness, such love . . . 'Come on, Mum!'

'It's true,' said Caroline. 'It's all true! She had done what to an adolescent is unforgivable . . . she had shown me up in front of my peers. It wasn't till years later that I was able to look back and forgive – and appreciate just what it must have cost her. At the time I could only think of what it had cost *me* – the shame it had brought me.'

'But nonetheless you returned to school afterwards, just as your heroine does?'

'I had to. I didn't want to; I was blackmailed into it. My mother pointed out that if I didn't go back it would mean she was responsible for ruining my life – the very life she'd struggled so hard to make normal for me. So I had to. There wasn't anything brave about it. I hated my last few terms. Everyone was so determinedly *nice* – and I just knew that behind the façade they were all congratulating themselves on how terribly decent they were being.'

It's true, if I look back: we were. We all felt genuinely sorry for Caroline, of course, but secretly we did consider that it was rather decent of us to behave in such a civilised fashion. People at *real* snob schools might have looked down on her, but not us! God, how smug we were. No wonder, once she'd kicked the dust from her heels she never came back.

'But you see,' she said, as they wound up the interview, 'I really *do* owe everything to my mother . . . everything I am, everything I've ever achieved . . . I have her to thank for it. I just wish – '

For a moment it seemed that the cool, calm voice of the professional actress faltered in its stride. (*Caroline*? Crying?)

'I just wish I could have told her while I still had the opportunity . . . Mum, I love you! Because I did . . . so much! So very much. Even this book – ' She gave a little laugh: under control once again. 'Without her, it could never have been written.'

I thought of sending a letter to Caroline, care of

the BBC, but I'm not sure that she would want to hear from me. I shall certainly go to the next reunion, now that I have news; though I daresay by then, since she has won this prize, everyone will already know.

The other day, just out of curiosity, I asked my daughter, 'What would *you* do if I were to turn up at Parents' Day and make a fool of myself?'

She said, 'We don't have a Parents' Day.'

'Well, all right! Open Day – Sports Day – *any* day! Would you come to my rescue?'

'You must be joking!' she said. 'I'd pretend I didn't know you . . .'

No One Else Will Do

JACQUELINE WILSON

I've never really got on with my mum. She's always made much more fuss of my brothers. You'd have thought she'd have liked a daughter after three boys on the trot. There's a photo on the top of the television taken when I was just a baby. Our family, all spruced up in our best clothes, squashed together on to a studio couch. Dad has a determined grin, lips peeled back to the gums. Jeff's grinning too, which is a mistake because his front teeth are missing. Danny is swinging his legs in the air, fidgeting them out of focus. Mike is pouting, pulling a face because he wants to be on Mum's lap. I'm there instead in my Christening frock, bald as an egg and bawling my head off.

'Three boys with lovely curls, and then you came along, Lizzie, and you didn't grow so much as a wisp until you were well past crawling. And look at that expression. Talk about temper! Always yelling, no matter what. There was no pleasing you.'

It looked as if there was no pleasing my mum either. She seemed to expect the boys to be grubby and untidy and didn't fuss them too much. She was always dabbing at me, wiping round my face with a wet flannel and buttoning me up so tight I could scarcely breathe. My hair eventually grew in straggly and straight. Mum tweaked it into a pony tail every morning, slicking it back so stiffly I couldn't even frown. It would work loose during the day, strands escaping all over the place, so that whenever I came home Mum would moan, 'Just look at the state of your hair, Lizzie!'

She only ever worked part-time so she was always there when we came home from school. She fussed us with mugs of milk and marmite sandwiches and little fairy cakes, but sometimes I wished I was a latchkey kid coming back to an empty kitchen. She'd ask us all about our day and she'd always tell me I could come top of the class like Jeff if I'd only try a bit harder. She'd smile as she watched Danny kick a ball about the garden and call me an old lazybones because I wanted to sprawl on the floor and watch the television. She pinned all Mike's paintings up on the kitchen wall but she sighed at mine and kept telling me to colour more carefully so that I didn't go over the lines.

I sometimes felt as if Mum had a black outline of an ideal daughter fixed in her mind – only I'd coloured myself in all wrong. I seemed to go over my own lines more and more the older I got.

'Look at all that tarty make-up! No wonder you're spotty, you silly girl.'

'You're not wearing a skirt like that, madam! You let that hem down at once.'

'You're going to twist your ankle in those shoes. You can hardly walk in them, let alone dance. And you're too young to go out to discos anyway. You should stay in and concentrate on your homework, young lady, not waste your time running after boys.'

I had to run hard after Mark. I didn't meet him

at a disco. He hates dancing, even though he'll skip about when he's in training. Danny brought him home to tea after football practice. I'm used to all my brothers bringing pals to tea – but Mark was different. Maybe it was the way his fair hair fell over his forehead. Maybe it was his big brown eyes. Maybe it was the way he smiled at me when he passed me the salt. I wanted him to go on passing me that salt until my spaghetti bolognaise was sprinkled snow white.

There was only one thing for it. I had to develop an overwhelming interest in football. I spent hours and hours on that boring, muddy field, cheering myself hoarse. I listened endlessly to their talk of tactics. It looked as if my own tactics were pretty ineffective at first. Mark hardly noticed me. I was just Danny's kid sister, the funny little tomboy who seemed mad on football. So I decided to reverse all the roles and I walked him home one day. I spent ages waffling: 'Well. Goodbye. Goodbye then. See you. Bye then, Mark' – and then I suddenly reached up and kissed him right on the lips before making a dash for home.

Mark came calling for me the next day and that was it. We were a couple after that.

Dad didn't mind too much. He said Mark was a nice lad and he talked five minutes' football with him every time he came to call for me.

Mum minded a lot.

'Why do you have to start going steady at your age, you silly girl? You're much too young for that sort of caper.'

I didn't think I was too young. I thought the beautiful things Mark and I were doing up in his bedroom were very grown-up indeed. We always pushed his chest of drawers against the door so we wouldn't get caught out. But we got caught out after all.

I think I knew I was in trouble right away but I couldn't face up to it. I let the weeks go past, pretending it wasn't happening. Maybe it was all a mistake. Maybe it was all going to be magically all right. I did really daft things, setting myself tasks like counting every book in the school library or not saying a single word to anybody all day, telling myself that if I could do it then I'd be OK. Mark knew something was troubling me but it took him ages to work it out. Then it dawned on him.

'Hey, Liz. There's nothing really wrong, is there? I mean, you're not having a baby, are you?'

'You got it in one,' I said, patting my tummy and trying to laugh. 'A little baby. And we're its mum and dad.'

Mark swallowed. He looked as if he might be going to burst into tears. Then he mumbled, 'I don't know what my mum's going to say.'

I'd pretended to myself that somehow he might make it all right. He'd tell me he loved me and that in spite of everything he was glad because it meant we would always belong together and that this was our destiny. I never dreamed he'd simply fuss about his mum.

I didn't know what my mum was going to say either. I knew I had to tell her but I didn't dare. I waited and waited. I told Mark I was waiting for an appropriate moment. There aren't any moments when it's appropriate to tell your mum you're going to have a baby.

But then one day Mum started nagging at me to go on a diet because I was getting so tubby. I burst into tears and she got tetchy with me, telling me not to be so sensitive, she was only trying to help me.

'You can't help me,' I sobbed. And then I told her.

Mum sighed. She always sighs like that when I'm around her. Somehow that was weirdly reassuring. She shut her eyes tight for a moment, as if she wanted to wish me away. But then she opened them again. She took a good long look at me.

'I might have known it,' she said, grimly. 'You silly little fool. How could you be so daft, eh? And nowadays, when there's just no excuse.'

'We slipped up,' I mumbled.

'I should say you did,' said Mum. 'Has Mark told his parents?'

'Not yet. He's scared they'll be furious.'

'Of course they'll be furious. A bright boy like that. They're set on him going to college. He's got his whole future in front of him. And so have you. Oh, Lizzie, trust you to make a mess of things.' She shut her eyes again. She kneaded her forehead with her fingers, and managed to smooth herself back into composure. 'Oh well. What's done is done. We'd better tell your dad. And the boys.'

'Oh, Mum. No. I can't.'

'You can. We can.'

The boys weren't too bad. Jeff even gave me a hug. Danny shuffled from one foot to the other and didn't seem too surprised. Maybe Mark had told him. Mike went very red and made a few stupid remarks until Mum got sharp and shut him up.

Mum told Dad for me, though she made me be there while she did it.

'Our Lizzie?' Dad whispered, bewildered. 'But she's only a kid herself.'

'Well, she's going to be a mother, even so.'

'It's all that boy's fault!'

Mark's mum thought it was all *my* fault. There was this terrible meeting between the six of us, Mark and me and the two sets of parents. Soon to be three sets of parents. Mark's mum said this was because I'd seduced her precious son. Dad started ranting and raving then, actually threatening Mark – though Mark is two inches taller than my dad and very fit from all that football training.

It was my mum who sorted it all out.

'What does it matter who did what? They're both stupid little idiots but that's nothing new. Come on, we've got to decide what's to be done.'

I didn't really have much choice. I'd waited so long I had to go through with having the baby now. Mark and I were still much too young to live together, let alone marry. So he carried on more or less as normal. Going to school. Going to football practice. Playing football at the weekends. I soon stopped going to school and stopped seeing most of my friends and stopped seeing Mark every night. I stayed in. I did lessons with a special tutor. I knitted. Mum taught me. I wasn't very good at it. Plain and purl stitch, and even that was such a struggle the white wool turned grey.

Then I went into hospital, clambering into the ambulance in one of Mum's old Laura Ashley smocks and my own school blazer, already in tears though it hadn't even started to hurt very much. I was so scared, that was why I was crying. Mark had promised he'd come with me but he was at school and although we left a message he didn't turn up until gone six, when the baby was already born.

Mum stayed with me. She held my hand and she wiped my forehead and she rubbed my back. When the pain got so bad I couldn't bear it she sang very softly in my ear. Lullabies, old love songs, even hymns, anything she could think of. She must have sung that way for me when I cried as a baby. Now I was having my own baby and she sang just the same. I cried as I pushed the baby out at last and Mum cried too. Then I held my little girl, so red and damp and strange. I'd never seen her before and yet I already loved her no matter what.

Mum smiled at both of us though her tears were still spilling down her cheeks and smudging her mascara.

'A little girl!'

My little girl, even though Mum looks after her for me while I'm at school. She gave up her job in the shop to stay home and look after Liza.

'Are you sure you don't mind, Mum?'

'Of course I mind. But it can't be helped, can it? And it's not as if I'm giving up some great career.'

'Well, it's just for a couple of years. We'll get Liza into nursery school. Then you can go back to the shop. Or – or train to do something else maybe?'

'At my age? No, you're the one who's got to do the training, Lizzie. I want you to have the career.'

'Maybe I'll marry Mark and have more babies.'

I still see Mark, but somehow it's not the same. He comes round to our house to see Liza some-times, generally when Dad's at work. We've been out together too, but we don't make love any more. We don't even seem to have that much to say to each other nowadays. I want to keep on loving him and believing that we might settle down together one day but I keep noticing stupid things like a new spot on his chin or the way he chews the little flakes of skin off his bottom lip, and somehow it's hard remembering we're supposed to be in love.

'There's more to life than staying home and having babies,' says Mum. 'I should know.'

'Why did you have four then, one after the other?'

'I don't know. You're not the only one who can slip up. And I wanted to keep on trying for a girl.'

'You wanted a girl? But you've always made such a fuss of the boys.'

'Maybe I was always stricter with you because you meant more.'

That set me back a bit. Does she really mean it? She still sighs and niggles and nags at me all the time. We have endless rows over little Liza. We both think we know the best way to feed her and change her and get her to sleep.

'I've brought up four babies, Lizzie. I do know what I'm talking about.'

'I know. But Liza's *my* baby.'

My Liza. My daughter. I hoped she'd have lovely fair hair like Mark, but she's bald as an egg, and she bawls a lot of the time. But she smiled for the first time today, when I got home from school. She smiled specially for me. I'm going to take over from Mum as soon as I can. I want to bring Liza up myself. Little girls need their mums. No one else will do.

The Authors

Anne Fine has won the Carnegie Medal for *Goggle-Eyes* and the Smarties Prize and the Nottinghamshire Library Oak Award for *Bill's New Frock*, which was also highly commended for the Carnegie Medal. Her latest book for Methuen is *The Angel of Nitshill Road*. She writes: 'I suspect there's a major design fault in the relationship between mothers and daughters. If it goes normally, everything seems to snarl up (often quite literally!). If it runs too smoothly, without any apparent snags or breakdowns, that's more a sign that something's wrong than that everything's going right. For the tempestuous side of things, try reading my *Book of the Banshee*.* But here, I've chosen to write about one of the peaceful times. Often there aren't that many, so it's good to make the best of them.'

* Hamish Hamilton.

Berlie Doherty won the Carnegie Medal for *Granny was a Buffer Girl* and has just published her first adult novel, *Requiem*, to much critical acclaim. It, too, contains moving and sensitive insights into a relationship between a mother and daughter. She writes: 'When I was growing up I found it very difficult to talk to my mother about the things that really mattered to me. Now I realise that it was because I couldn't imagine her being a young person herself. In my novels for teenagers, *Granny was a Buffer Girl, White Peak Farm* and *Dear Nobody*, I explore the idea of a teenager coming to understand herself through understanding her mother. In *Shrove Tuesday* it's the mother who understands herself through her daughter.'

Vivien Alcock's *The Monster Garden* was shortlisted for the Whitbread, Carnegie and Smarties awards. *The Trial of Anna Cotman* was commended for the Carnegie Medal. Her most recent book – very much about fathers and daughters – is *A Kind of Thief*. She writes: 'Mothers and daughters are like loving hedgehogs; full of warmth and tenderness and prickles. I understand my own mother better now that I'm a mother myself, and know how much I love, worry about, fuss over, am proud of, delight in and sometimes exasperate my own daughter Jane, just as my mother did with me.'

Jamila Gavin is much praised for her books about children who find themselves part of two cultures. In *The Singing Bowls* she wrote superbly about fathers and sons. She writes: 'Perhaps the hope of every mother with a daughter is that the parent/ child relationship will develop into both of them becoming the best of friends, on equal terms.

In the story, *I Want to be an Angel*, the close, caring friendship between mother and daughter seems to be indestructable. There is no hint of the cloud of impending adolescence which can cast a blight on the very best relationship, as in *Forbidden Clothes*, when the shadows fall in the form of rebellion.'

Marjorie Darke is rightly acclaimed for her novel about the suffragettes, *A Question of Courage*. She writes: 'Being a daughter and the mother of a daughter, I treasure this special relationship with its complex tugs of love, tears, friendship, fun, resentment and much else, yet only once before have I written about it – overflowing into two books! Emily and her mother live in Birmingham's backstreets at the turn of the century; Emily leaving as World War One approaches (*A Question of Courage, A Rose from Blighty*). Vastly different in experience from Kelly and her mum. But many of us share similarities of feeling, no matter where we live, or whether the year is 1912, 1992, even 2002!'

Gwen Grant is acclaimed for the warmth and humour of *The Lily Pickle Eleven*, and for her poignant portrayals of very real struggles and the relationships which evolve through them. She writes: 'I now understand more clearly the power and complexity of the relationship between mother and daughter. As we grow older, some part of the bond has to be broken and a new equality established. It is this relationship of love and frustration that is explored in my book, *The Revolutionary's Daughter*.'

Annie Dalton was shortlisted for the Carnegie Medal for her second novel, *Night Maze*. She has won the Nottinghamshire Library Oak Award for *The Afterdark Princess*. She writes: 'I can't seem to stop writing about mothers and daughters: a single-parent duo in *Out of the Ordinary*, a fraught adoptive relationship in *Night Maze* and *two* sets in

The Alpha Box when I meant to keep them out
entirely. So it was a relief to be asked to write an
official M and D story. All mothers and daughters
have mixed feelings about each other. Generally
mothers follow one script and daughters another.
And the only sane response to that baffling chasm
between the two is mad hoots of laughter – as here
in *A Werewolf in May*.'

Monica Hughes is a prize-winning author of
fantasy and science fiction. Her compelling Isis
trilogy begins with *The Keeper of the Isis Light* and she
has recently published *Invitation to the Game*. She
writes: 'Mothers and daughters: a relationship that
can be as close as best friends – or it can be
dynamite because each sees reflected in the other
both the best and worst aspects of herself.

'The strongest relationship between mother and
daughter in any of my books is in the most recent,
The Crystal Drop. The mother is dead on page one of
the story, but it is her image and the memory of her
strength that gives Megan the courage to set out
with her younger brother on an impossible
journey.'

Jean Ure won the Lancashire Book Award for
Plague 99 and will shortly publish its sequel, *Come
Lucky April*. She writes: 'The mother/daughter
relationship, although one of the most important in
the lives of almost all women, has not been
explored nearly as often as it should in fiction for
young people.

'Mothers figure prominently in much of my own
writing, as do daughters, but in only one set of

books, the Abe and Marianne trilogy, have I tackled the relationship between the two – between, in this case, prickly, rebellious Marianne and sensible, understanding, but by no means perfect Mrs Fenton.'

Jacqueline Wilson is the author of many successful books for young people. Her ability to write about difficult situations with sensitivity and insight has won her much praise. She writes: 'My mum didn't hang about the house in a pinny when I was little. She went out to work in a smart suit and came home with cream buns and comics. She was special. She still is. My daughter Emma used to play that she was a lady called Angela and I was a lady called Rosie and we were Best Friends. Now Emma's grown up and we're women, not ladies, but we're still Best Friends.

'I often write about mothers and daughters (particularly in *The Other Side, Amber* and *The Dream Palace*) but I don't put my own mother or daughter in my books. I want us to stay special, to be Best Friends forever.'

In Between

First kisses, standing up for other people and making decision's on one's own. Eleven funny, sad and brave stories about growing-up, reflecting the moment when childhood is left behind.

The prize-winning and best-selling contributors are : Vivien Alcock, Rachel Anderson, Joanna Carey, Adèle Geras, Elizabeth Laird, Sam McBratney, Michael Morpurgo, Alick Rowe, Ian Strachan, Robert Westall and Jacqueline Wilson.

"An excellent collection . . . A must . . ."
School Librarian

"Strong, involving stories."
Junior Bookshelf

"A strong and interesting collection . . ."
Books for Keeps

EDITED BY MIRIAM HODGSON

Love Hurts

In this superb collection of 24 stories, love is portrayed in all its many guises with realism and humour.

Featuring stories by Vivien Alcock, Annie Dalton, Marjorie Darke, Berlie Doherty, Adèle Geras, Mary Hooper, Monica Hughes, Mollie Hunter, Pete Johnson, David Johnstone, Geraldine Kaye, Jenny Koralek, Anthony Masters, Jenny Nimmo, Michael Pearson, Joan Phipson, Ann Pilling, Alison Prince, Dyan Sheldon, Ian Strachan, Jean Ure and Diana Wynne Jones with a foreward by K M Peyton, winner of the Carnegie Medal.

A bumper collection of stories previously available in three volumes - *The Teens Book of Love Stories*, *Heartache* and *Take Your Knee Off My Heart*.